A SCATTERED LOOK AT

HARASSMENT ARCHITECTURE

A BOOK BY MIKE MA

D1739017

A SCATTERED LOOK AT

HARASSMENT ARCHITECTURE

A BOOK BY MIKE MA

WARNING

I preface this all with a reminder that none of what you're about to read reflects upon the author himself. The following is purely fiction.

For your enhanced reading experience, I have marked chapters and pieces I value most. It's for those people who don't read entire books. Or those people who don't give a shit about everything I say. Or for those who are coming back for more.

They are denoted by a tiny "x" following chapter titles.

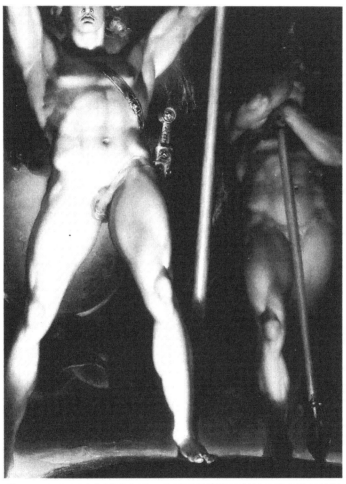

I STAND AT THE BRIDGE BETWEEN YOU AND THE REMAINDER OF AN UNFULFILLING LIFE

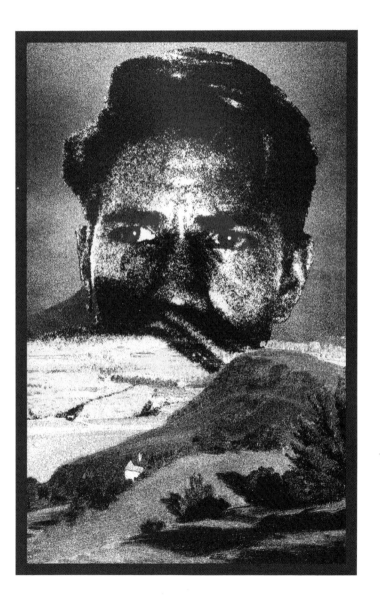

SECOND WARNING

If you came here expecting coherent plot or structure, you bought or stole the wrong book.

[New author's note: Having finished the second book, I decided to revisit this one. I am impressed with how bad it is. What you are about to read is the second edition. I have fixed as much as I could.]

Dedicated to CT, HN, BC, WM, BG, BAP, BM, etc

OPENING

At the end of it all, in those darkest of days,
smiles man atop the mountain debris.
He can see the many stars, smell the coming wind,
only now does he know that he's free.

I'm listening to Wagner's *Tannhäuser* with the windows down. Mostly because I want the people at this red light to know I'm a cultured guy. A girl of about eighteen, probably soon graduating high school, pulls up on my left. She's trying desperately to avoid eye contact and undeniably scared by the atmosphere I've crafted along this ride. I'm broadcasting this kind of unhinged but handsome white male wavelength. A kind of manic superbreakdown in waiting. Hidden behind knock-off Ray-Bans are two tired, bloodshot eyes. They sting as if this world was a chlorinated pool, and so I'm made to hide them. She keeps pivoting her head more and more in the opposite direction until I call her "bitch" at my loudest. Now she's just nervous-angry. As for me? I look good today, so naturally the consequence of certain actions is reduced by half or more.

It's not usually like this. I'm not usually so on edge, so forthright. I'm not usually exhaling death pheromones into the common man's air. I'm not usually foaming at the mouth. But today, I feel the blood flowing with a little more ease. I've felt like this for a while now. Weeks maybe. Months possibly. I believe that my brain is getting more oxygen than normal. Perhaps it's my increase in both raw meat and milk consumption. Anyone else would say they feel alive if suddenly put in my shoes, but I feel only the polar opposite. I feel like I am dead. Dead, roaming but not rotting among this downward-pointed Earth. I am bound by zero consequence and terrified for everyone around me. I'm not worried for myself though, because I'm quickly accepting that whatever happens to me, however bad it may be, is supposed to happen. Admittedly, this is due to some light spiritual reading I've done as of late. Parts of the genre are wise, other parts are horseshit. I've only lightly sprinkled the new knowledge into my grander worldview. The next step is to understand my role in this reign of terror, to see find my place in the shifting of this world.

I now have the volume turned up to its loudest with the windows still down because I'm feeling some ancestral renegade blood aflush. The occasional odd look makes me consider turning the music down but it also doesn't. I am a violent and screeching engine, shaking and tapping on the leather-bound steering wheel. On the opposite end of this geographical location is another me, a carbon copy of myself, pounding a cow skin drum in the rain. He's my antipodal clone. Regardless of my new life decisions, there's a shred of self-consciousness hidden somewhere deep inside me. It never wins. I'm sitting at the same red light, watching the same girl I just harassed as she inches forward and forward a little more. She's now touching the bumper of the truck ahead. I almost feel bad for her until I realize she didn't understand my humor. She truly is a bitch.

The light finally turns green and, excitedly, I gas too hard, smashing the rear end of the Prius ahead. Initially, I don't realize this until the schmuck inside jumps out and starts yelling over my blaring car stereo. He's wearing a ponytail and jean shorts with some unrecognizable band tee. KISS, maybe? Faggot. He's approaching my window, still screaming and so I peel out and down the nearest right. And yes, I'm not a scumbag, I checked if there was any significant damage to his car beforehand – there was, that's why I left.

Do not worry. The whole story isn't like this. I won't continue to narrate completely standard days. It gets better, you son of a bitch. I hope at least a few of these words make you want a long walk. Or a cigarette outside. Maybe you'll start a farm on mortgaged land. Or maybe you'll start screen-printing tee shirts. The government could provide you free land in exchange for clams you collect on its shores. You could bomb logging trucks. You could sell drums of destroy-everything oil. Learn to sculp. Learn to read. Any of these things, as a result of this story.

There's a concert tonight and the few friends I've got here have invited me to come out. They aren't my real friends though, mostly because I can't be racist, sexist, or myself around them. I feel a tension in my stomach when I think about going, but in reality, nothing about the night makes me anxious. The opinions of all the people I'll be with and the others around us is completely meaningless to me. Whatever, moving on. I am too young to formulate respectable opinions of the world, so I don't expect anyone to take me seriously. I'm rambling, and someone is listening, even if it isn't you. That someone is either more naive than I am, or much smarter and enjoying the pompous sting. On the record, I'll regret all of this someday. Off the record, I'm pretty certain I won't.

I take it back — any faux-existentialist worry I've given off. It is all so gauche, so heavy-handed. I refuse to ingest the pill of doom. And I refuse to push it, either. I also refuse to associate with queer nihilists who think they know something the rest of us haven't figured out. Fuck you, you don't. Even if you did, nobody would care because you're too busy guzzling Sutter Home to industry-plant rappers on the balcony of your off-campus apartment. Keep buying vinyl, that's definitely a good investment, retard. You read the words "God is dead," online and didn't investigate its context any further? That's very interesting and I would love to hear more. You know what's dead? Pretending to care about minorities, makeup tutorials, talking about politics, and astrology. It's hard to take someone seriously when they've become fanatical over something truly undeserving. You're crying about a cable show? You still watch shows? You still have cable? How fucking dull. Pick something with more merit. Maybe get sickly attached to New Order or emotionally handcuff yourself to a death cult in the middle of Iowa. For bonus points, pick something from actual obscurity — and no, not Bauhaus. You stand before a sign that says, "cum is Ggod," also known as "pay attention to me, I'm a different kind of slut". Kick out your car's rear windshield, tie a chain around both a lamppost and your neck. Leave a respectable amount of slack. Drive forward and fast.

Someone I work with told me about this guy from his hometown who, upset by a breakup, drove his truck into a gas station pump at full speed while blowing his head off with a shotgun. Yes, all at the same time. Part of me believes it wasn't so much the breakup that caused it, but more so living in upstate New York.

Anyways. I was talking about the concert and got off track. It's a "post-hardcore, post-rock" band which essentially means the songs are ten minutes longer than normal and someone with a beard and flannel will be playing the violin. It's in a bar too, so I get to watch people pay seven-fifty for a Blue Moon that'll just get dropped when the tempo ramps up. Everyone starts bouncing and into the floor's black void it will fall. A pool of beer forms around everyone's feet and by the end, they all sink in and die.

I don't like the people at these types of shows. Or at any concert really. Are they all "nice"? Sure, whatever that means. There is a certain aspect to them that has me constantly examining myself, checking that I don't become the same. It's not only that I don't want to dress the same, or adopt the same body language. It's not just their political opinions and dismal outlooks. I'm just focused primarily on me not belonging here.

I'd much rather enjoy these songs alone in the dark or in the company of better people. Yes, how withdrawn and unique of me to say such a thing. Get over yourself.

I am at the concert and the concert is full of people I don't like at the concert. I am at the concert and I am smirking in the corner, ignoring what my peers are discussing. Let us picture something good. I'm wearing a level-two bulletproof vest under my Ralph Lauren vintage flannel, and already it's almost entirely concealed. Makes me look slightly more built, nobody's complaining. It also protects against nine millimeter and forty caliber rounds, the only kinds police use anymore. I think. Over that, a Swiss military jacket, littered with pockets, all of which I custom fit to hold the six magazines accompanying my short barrel rifle. It's a gun small enough to fit perfectly along my back while still under my coat. In the pockets of my Levi five-elevens – a switchblade and one smoke grenade, reserved for either my entrance or exit. I still haven't decided. In my waistband is a…

…and then two squad cars skid to a halt outside. I see them before they see me, as the front windows are tinted in my favor. With a fresh magazine, I aim and shoot at –

"HEY!"

Someone shouting playfully in my face has yanked me back into the concert hall and everyone is alive. Here, I and my sorrows stand. Alone, brushing from my shoulder the tiny shattered pieces of a black dream. Of course, it's only a little alternative humor. Dark jokes, new age comedy. Shootings are a waste of time anyways. That or they are CIA operations.

"You want something from the bar?" the girl asks me, smiling.

She must be one of my "friend's" friends because I do not recognize her.

"I don't drink, thanks though," I reply, nose upturned.

She smiles and nods in a goofy manner, then turns for the bar. I turn too, confusedly, back towards the stage. I try for even a short moment to ease back into that violent daydream, but it has passed and with it my desire to be here. Faking for this long has left me drained of my cultivated vril. Complaining for this long has left me tired. One of these days, I'll form a pact with myself – no complaining, ever. Each one costs a lashing.

The drink-retrieving girl returns to our little powwow and she's asking me where I work. I lie to her quietly, hoping the others don't hear and correct me. Drink girl now believes that I'm big on Wall Street, and I have learned that she's going to veterinarian school. Actually, she may have said nursing school. Every whore wants to be a nurse. Drink girl is riddled in bruises and ugly tattoos. Some of her tattoos even look like bruises. It's domestic violence-chíc tonight at the music show. At this point in the conversation she's expressed a sexual interest in me and bashfully notes that she's been "stalking" me for a while. I laugh and excuse myself to the bathroom.

When I come back, the first band has started and the crowd is totally impartial. It's some local group of dickheads with sailor tattoos singing about their ex-girlfriends. I spin around to survey the crowd and accidentally catch the eyes of that stupid fucking girl in doing so. Not only that, but the band ends their set just then. How romantic, for her.

More conversation, more of me lying about generally meaningless things. She wouldn't be bad looking if she wasn't so bad looking. I have no interest in this five-foot-five dead end and so I excuse myself again, this time outside. I can see my car down the road and it's calling for me to drive it home. I do.

My "friends" are calling me to see where I went. I don't answer,

13

and quickly decide I won't be seeing them again. I'm young and I'm making rash, destructive decisions.

DON'T GO TO NEW YORK CITY_x

It's another day and I'm in New York City for work. This place is the type of shithole that would frustrate me into an early grave granted I couldn't find the words to describe it. It was not desire, but a small job contract that led me here. Looking out the window of this cafe makes me nauseous. The entire city makes me nauseous. I can feel my skin crawling with the spittle of not just any kind of people, but New Yorkers – a special degree of bad. I space out. Thrown into my own head, I'm searching for anything else to feel.

I'd like to live in the nineties. Not the actual nineties, but the one that my generation and others have made up. We imagined this version of it, so heavily romanticized for decades in conversation and movies; music and art. Many of us were born just short of experiencing it, and because of that, we rebuilt it in our heads forever onwards. Capitalism was a friend, Kurt Cobain fueled already mounting angst among high school kids, and the racial divide just didn't seem to exist. Honestly, I don't give a shit about that last part. Whether or not any of what I said is true is irrelevant, because it's our vision, and so it becomes true. It's our recollection of "back then," and you couldn't change it even if you tried. People do try, all the time. Bitter children of the real nineties are always twitching to correct the vision, like hall monitors or war veterans or something. They never win. Our vision, not theirs.

We push on, tying flannels around our waists, ripping holes into pairs of ill-fitting jeans. We'll knock things down in the mall and listen to the new Smashing Pumpkins record in someone's father's car. Our parents will shoot us looks of disgust when we come home for dinner, smelling faintly of cigarettes and fast food. We'll sleep like angels to the sound of leaves blowing down crime-free suburban streets. There's nothing that can touch us; we live our lives like an old Disney Channel movie. Not even Columbine could happen here. We'll make out in public parks, steal some candy bars, and run like someone actually cares. We'll skate past the girls tanning on the beach. Our hair styled perfectly by saltwater and sun. Blonde and brown bangs in our eyes. Bodies chiseled from marble, a result of paddling out into head-high waves and pushing steel around after school. Sun children with sun skin from sun worship, skin clear from the same. It's like this forever because those visions replay forever. It's like this for as long as we want this. Forever.

We'll graduate high school, go to university, and marry super pretty girls. We'll try drugs, and experience those television movie hardships. Some of us won't stop trying drugs and die in gas stations like pathetic deadbeats. Those people simply dissolve from the vision. The rest of us die of old age, some with grandchildren who ask us about what the nineties were like. Some with grandchildren that know we're excited to tell them.

There was a time when me and all my friends lived in something like this. It wasn't too close, but just close enough to where our minds would fill in the blanks. That romanticized, surrogate world would leak dreamily into the real. The result was wholesome. It is something I think back on whenever reminded. I feel bad for people who didn't walk away with the same feeling, the same kind of memories, the same sense of nothing left undone. Especially since it's not hard to have achieved.

Someone I must have met before walks into the cafe I'm daydreaming in. I say this because she keeps glancing at me with what I perceive as hopeful eyes. She's made a gesture towards me that I haven't yet accepted, and so she floats in that sea of uncomfortable doubt. Everyone around her watches. I put my glasses on, realizing now that I do actually know her. I wave back to signal her over.

Her name is Dolores and I've always wondered why she didn't use Dorothy, a much prettier name, instead. She sits across from me and I push down the screen of my computer to take her in. She smiles and asks me why I'm in the city with a gentle, interested tone. She has a voice that doesn't belong to New York City because when she speaks, you aren't suddenly coated in poison acid. You don't flinch and dodge reptilian phlegm throughout your conversation.

"Just work. I couldn't do it from home, sadly."

She tells me about an internship she started; about how stressful city life is, about how much she drinks. About how the drinking is no longer confined to the weekends but now includes weeknights too; sometimes even mornings to alleviate the aforementioned. She tells me about her roommate who she just can't get along with. I nod. She talks about student loans and the political climate. I nod again. She talks. I nod.

I'm not disinterested by her, I'm just recovering from a rich daydream of another life. The more she goes on, the deeper I fall into my own liquid image, more so than usual. This fantasy is fermented; it digests slowly and without any strain on the system. You look forward to it throughout more than days, but an entire lifetime. It's a dessert, dense in both texture and nutrition. A lot of these recent daydreams have felt like this. Anything can make you feel full, but few things can fill you without regret.

This conversation needs an end. I shut my computer, signaling departure, and she understands the reason why. I don't want to make it seem as if I'm in a rush, because I'm not. I just prefer not to be here, specifically here, any longer. I walk down forty eighth and Madison and stop inside a hotel lobby to check flight reservations. I'm leaving the city because it's disgusting. Did I mention I'm now crawling with alien spittle.

I am fucking sick of this place and again left wondering why I bother coming at all. No amount of money is worth the visit.

There's something sinister about New York City that I've never felt in any other place on Earth. It goes beyond the resting heart rate of panic, and beyond the general disgust. New York City reeks of more than just hot homeless garbage piss — it reeks of guilt and fear and so much else. It's a city that dove too deeply, too quickly into the world of technology and the idea of a melting pot, then realized how empty that future felt. Occasionally, they'll try to claw their way back to former days, but can only poorly mimic them. Burger shacks that rely solely on iPads as cash registers, that cook their food using intentionally-dated stoves and tools. Manic NYU students in ugly sweatshop sweatpants, staring into their twenty-dollar minimalist salads, sitting uncomfortably at rustic wood tables, artificially banged up by crafty Chinatown merchants. Every new dent is another twenty-five dollars onto the asking price. Not a single smoothie shop CEO bothers to argue. They love the look and even write pridefully about it in their Moleskine day journals. What fucking losers. A city of queers buying anything that looks like it came from a tree because they haven't actually seen one in a lifetime. Did you know the trees in Central Park are made of ultra-dense recycled plastics? That's why they don't break, even when some intel-funded creature sets off explosives on passing joggers.

Everyone in New York will rave for hours about how much they love it. Their favorite clubs, their favorite musicals, their favorite streets to avoid because a friend got stabbed and raped there last March. If you listen long enough, they start to whittle down into a much truer form, a kind of terror hidden under giddiness. New York City's native population and veteran residents are a bunch of neurotic slimy rodents, one giant gang of life's rejects. Sick and twisted faggots with nothing but venom in their bodies. The entire city, in every single aspect, is a grift. Everything is obtained through immoral means — and not even the cool kind. Jews having ten kids to avoid property tax, Chinamen selling knockoff designer handbags, mystery meat business creeps atop skyscrapers thinking about which forest to next destroy. At least in Los Angeles they own their vapidity. New York City and the rats that nest inside its many holes try so hard to believe they're in touch with reality. They pride themselves on being citypeople, on not being a fly-over state redneck. The next fifty bombings won't wake them up and the next couple twelve-dollar packs of Parliaments won't either. The people of New York are like fragile soap carvings and I am an unexpected torrential downpour. Watch for streets full of bubbles, and then streets full of nothing, except remnants of trash. There's only one thing to separate the Big Apple from any third-world favela and it's perception. Also known as lying to yourself.

The Soho Grand is the latest hot location for the worst the city has to offer. Screeching faggots, drug addict club promoters, lecherous 'daddy's money' cunts. The main room is easily accessible because the building itself functions primarily as a hotel. It'd be a shame if someone went in, undetected, before clubbing hours, and coated the dance room in ██████████ ██████████. Better yet, coat the whole street, or city. Cover the entire city in ██████ and watch humanity rejoice. Some people would act upset at first, but after a while, they'd come to see why it was needed. It's not exactly like putting Ol' Yeller down, but close enough.

Did I mention everyone in New York City has at least one STD? I'm leaving. I hope to never again cross the north Virginia state line.

BLACK AND BLUE MONDAY

Getting my shit kicked in by a clan of Jewish boarding school kids for referring to the Torah as the *Elder Scroll*. Five or six of them repeatedly soccer-kicking my back and stomach in the Seven-Eleven parking lot. When it all ended, I noticed one of their hats had fallen off, and so I let him know. "My friend! Your beanie doth fell," and then they started kicking me all over again. I saw a couple of ambulances pass by, but they belonged to the local Hatzalah and would never rescue someone outside the faith. It's okay though; I stood up on my own. This is the kind of Monday I live for.

ROMANCIPATION'S HIGHWAY

Romanticism isn't buying flowers for your girlfriend. Romanticism is buying flowers for your girlfriends. Romanticism is getting into a knife fight with unbeatable odds. Romanticism is a gunshot victim dabbing his fingers into the wound, painting stripes on his face before the medics arrive. Romanticism is hunting down local gay dating app users and beating them with a phonebook or a sock full of coins. Romanticism is voluntary celibacy. Romanticism is baseball bat hate crimes. Romanticism is total debauchery or total anti-debauchery. Romanticism is sex, and sex is just a fight where you come at the end.

Romanticism could be none of these things. It varies. Maybe it's just whatever you feel it is. I realize I'm probably mouthing these words as they cross my mind because the woman next to me is moving inch-by-inch into her husband's lap.

What's in a name? That which we call a woman by any other name would still cause problems.

HOME'S BARBER

Now home, in the town in which I live, I enter the best-known local barber shop with a mess of blonde hair falling into my eyes. Long hair rarely looks good on me. The woman cutting it asks what I do for work. I have a little trouble answering because when she said it, I was busy screaming at the walls inside my head for letting a female style my hair. Every cut she makes is another I know I'll regret, but I'm in too deep and I have to let her finish.

"Where'd you say you work?" she asks again, a bit more direct. I must have mumbled something.
"I'm in a band. We just got done touring Europe."
"Well hey, look at you!" she's excited about the lie I just told.

There's a silence after this and to her it's probably nothing. I'm not immune to discomfort, as this conversation and the many others like it have proven. Maybe she knows I'm lying to her and now I just look fucking stupid. I might say the n-word, to be honest.

"So, where in Europe?" smacking her gum, making eye contact with me momentarily. I sigh in relief; the tone of her voice assures me the lie has been bought.
"Stockholm, Paris, Munich, all those sorts of places. We got stuck in vampire territory once, really scary – right downhill from a castle. I could have sworn I saw a man in a cape looking down at us. He was holding a giant sword, too. As soon as I told the guys, our driver got to fixing the bus a little faster. Hah. Working in no time!"

I'm thinking about taking the scissors she's butchering my hair with and putting them through her face. In between vocally guiding her and telling her specifically what she's fucking up, I am ready to lose it. The end has finally come and she's managed to make me look pretty good, not without my tireless help though. I'm pretty shocked. No I'm not. More so at myself for leaving with a haircut and not handcuffs.

I'm sitting outside on the terrace and an unexpected calmness washes over me. I'm looking at the trees and the birds in them, jumping from branch to branch. It looks like they're having more fun than myself. I need to shake my bad attitude. I'm looking at all of this through a different lens of emotion and it makes me think about how much I'd like to embrace nature and live in its purity. In the same thought, I'm aware that by the time I've driven out to a sizable piece of land with all the necessary tools to survive that I'll lose the ambition to follow that feeling. This limbo between a desire to return to the primal world and the realization that it isn't so easy gives me a sense of how deep I've fallen into my comfort zone. Both the Industrial and Agricultural Revolutions and their consequences have been a disaster for the human race. At any moment something could, and should, tear every last possession I have away. What's left is only the sun and what grows beneath it.

"It's only after you've lost everything that you're free to do anything."

At this point, the only resolution is for something to wash it all away, forcing me into the nearest flush of woods, feeding on the land and the animals I kill. Wash me all away, and this. How sad is it to desire such a thing? A system that was not that long ago a completely standard way of life. There are pieces and places of the world where it is still so – to enter them as a tainted modern man though, that's a cruel poison I'd never introduce.

I return to the happier, more previous train of thought. The one where I simply stared into the wild and admired. It's hard to talk about nature without sounding pretentious. You either start doing it and feel pretentious or someone calls you such. These desires I have to immerse myself in the ways of the past world are not an REI commercial. They are not an extended stay camping trip. They are not temporary.

No, I'm not Thoreau; I haven't exiled myself to a cut of barren woods and written down my findings. I'm just some son of a bitch sitting outside his home beside a beautiful piece of property. I don't care if I'm pretentious. Everything is pretentious when everyone is a nihilist. Everything is pretentious on the downwards pointed Earth. Everyone is all rotting and talk. There's no purity left to us here because the apathetic tailspinners have consolidated life into one big joke. Sincerity is dead or laughed at. That's why it's so peaceful inside the liquid dream, the thoughts that move inside me when I do. There are no twenty-something liberal arts majors to tell me that what I'm writing about comes off as hollow. They're hollow. Their personality is the legal intellectual property of a television series. They are ugly and expendable. They are burdens hiding in clearance rack mall clothes. They are the rape of the world.

There's a bright green pine tree directly in front of me. It's almost lime under the spring's honest sunlight, and behind it is another beautiful tree, coated in white flowers. To someone like me with horrible vision and no glasses on hand, the landscape becomes something else. The lime pine needles and the white flowers behind them blend into a remarkably soft gradient. Pattern recognition starts recognizing pattern recognition. Time becomes a flatter and flatter circle as it gets better. The you inside the circle gets better, wealthier, more advanced, but everything creeps back around and it's you versus old enemies again. Another pattern recognized. It loops all the way back to the first race. They were doing this too, they have done all that also. There's things of beauty where pessimism is displaced.

I'm torn from this daydream by someone peeling out in the distance. It doesn't take long before I fall back in. Like liquid, always. Right now, I am alone in this world. Sure I have friends and family. Sure I have past girlfriends and new sycophants. But here, in this rift, I am entirely alone and I feel it too. Here I'm crossing familiar fields with familiar people.

Looking up, I notice words written in the sky:

"YOU MAY NEVER GET TO SEE FIFTY FOOT STATUES OF WARLORDS AND EMPERORS. YOU MAY NEVER FEEL THE TRIUMPH OF CONQUEST. YOU MAY NEVER SEE MAN LIVE AS THE ANCIENTS DREAMED HE WOULD AND IT'S ALL BECAUSE A COUPLE OF RATS TUNNELED THEIR WAY INTO POSITIONS OF POWER. THEY SAID THE PAST IS WRONG. THEY SAID INVADERS SHOULD HAVE YOUR LAND. THEY SAID IT'S OKAY TO EMBRACE APATHY. YOU ARE A VICTIM OF THE TECHNOCRACY, OF AN ABUSE NAMED 'CIVILITY'. YOU HAVE BEEN ROBBED OF A FULFILLING, EARNEST LIFE. TAKE IT BACK, CUT THEIR THROATS."

It's not so bad to be alone. We put too much energy into always seeking the presence of another; especially men seeking women. I'd say it's unhealthy to spend too much time with other people. It would be trite to say I wish for a day where the world is empty and I'm the only one alive; it'd also be untrue. What I really wish for is a world in total chaos. I wish for the collapse of humanity as a result of everything we've done wrong. A world where everyone is too busy burning to bother you. Maybe I burn too, but it'll be alone.

Our lifetimes are akin to that feeling you get when you're having too much fun. Too much, too good, for too long. You sense that something very bad is just around the corner. You know this because it has happened before, maybe not to you, but to relatives or someone you read about. **The entire presence of industrialized man has been a violent preface to his looming and inescapable consequence. The final consequence.** I'm not the only one who feels this way, otherwise certain sects of Christianity wouldn't exist.

The timeline of humanity, since industrialization, is one long and wild drunk drive. A kind of victory lap[AI]. The moment I await is that telephone pole our driver can't see. We'll wrap around it at eighty miles per hour and the bodies will mesh together like room temperature cookie dough. The bones turn to dust from the sheer impact; the blood covers every exposed surface of the interior. The worst part of it all is that we remain completely aware of the pain as it happens – a very immediate and sensory leap into sin's scolding hot spring. We feel the steering wheel enter and then exit through the middle of our spines. We feel the windshield shatter in our eyes, pulverized into a blend of chunks and sand. We feel the fire charring off our skin as it litters the highway. I shouldn't say "we". Not me, I have no part in this. You. You people feel all of this. Maybe not you, maybe just the others. Me? I'm the lone driver of an entirely separate vehicle. One who only stumbles upon the wreckage. It brings me to a blush and grin. I get back into my car and leave.

Not long ago, I read that Christians invented guilt and that horrible, sinking feeling so often attached. I think we would have created guilt or guilt's accomplice regardless of religion's touch. I do not like it. I do not like to come across it, especially in moments I'd never foresee. I understand the concept of sin, and while not fully agreeing on the degrees of punishment, I believe it's there. Guilt, however, I don't know or want. Maybe it can be avoided. Maybe it can be erased. Do you know of a man who vanquished guilt?

We are the rapidly increasing rate of change over minimal time. We are the exponential climb towards a grand mass death. It goes and it goes and it goes.

PLEASURE SEEKER

"There are women you can marry and there are women you can't. The ones you can't are called whores and they've earned this title after emerging as veterans from the battlefield of male attention and casual sex." I explain to a friend.

"I just don't understand why they have to be categorized."

"It's really simple, there's nothing overly complex about this. They are categorized for your own good, really."

"I get it, I guess," he shrugs me off.

"Whores are a commodity. They are there when you need to unload pent up testosterone and, generally, they'll never interject themselves into your actual life, your actual relationships, or whatever else. This doesn't mean we shouldn't have a death squad that rounds them up for execution, it just means we should use them for what they're trained for until they are gone."

"I said I get it."

"I don't think you do. If we were headed in the direction God or whoever else intended, they'd be a thing of the past. But we aren't, and so we deal with them accordingly."

This conversation isn't going anywhere and I've become too passionate about something that ultimately doesn't even matter. I still want whores dead, this much I stand by. Again I find myself alone, only this time it's in a deli.

"Thots are a tragedy of the commons."

A REAL HUMAN VICTIM

I'm a victim of negativity and in that a victim of irony, of cultural poverty, and really, a victim of the institution. The people at the head of all that is evil want nothing more than for me to want nothing more. They want me and everyone around me in a state of indifference. They want us never to express sincerity because sincerity can inspire revolution. The majority moves left and so do we.

The minorities move left and I'm scared over to the right.

Nihilism and irony are really neat until you're dead and the only person who remembers you is your weed dealer. Nothing but a body, found only because it hadn't resupplied on drugs in a while. Imagine you are given the world only to pretend that you don't care about it. Imagine thinking Seinfeld is the single best show. This place is a miracle with indescribable beauty and I can't seem to appreciate it enough because I idolized the insincere for far too long. They've trained me in the dangerous ways of apathy for twenty-something years and I want it all to end. Saying that alone is a stand against it, but it isn't enough. I want to care, more, again. Not only as my last stand, but because I know the others will follow behind me if the cause is correctly chosen. I'm worried that everyone I know will reduce themselves to a shallow grave.

If anything, why not funnel your nihilism into something absurd and productive. You don't care about this place? Wonderful. Take a rifle and empty one entire drum magazine into the windows of ▓▓▓▓▓▓▓▓. Empty the magazine and don't look back unless everything in that hornet's nest is contaminated with lead. You don't care about anything? Let me write a message about something that pains me, tape it to your chest, and send you into ▓▓▓▓▓▓▓▓ for a memorable public self-execution. Let me cover you in plastic explosives and take you on a field trip to the largest power station in America.

[Please note: Do not do any of these things. Especially do not cover your face and destroy the many and largely unprotected power stations and cell towers. Electricity is a ghost, but one you can catch and kill. Do not do that. Do not become the sort of person who gets really good at blowing power stations up while never getting caught.]

I hear that migrants are being captured and sold as slaves in Libya, right now. It would be a shame if someone loaded up a cargo truck full of them, armed them all to the teeth, and let them loose in major cities around the UK and Europe. It would be a shame if you told these generally low-IQ individuals that killing large numbers of people would guarantee their freedom is returned. It would be a shame if you took this same concept, but loaded them into a cargo plane and let them loose in New York City, in Los Angeles. Let them loose outside of major news stations and the towers of international bankers.

As I said, do not do anything I say during these sorts of tirades. That you should believe in something now more than ever is probably sound advice though.

"The devil will find work for idle hands to do."

WELCOME TO IT ALL

Office building paintings were always the Gap models of art. Just enough to briefly catch the eye, if that, and never enough to seriously impress you. Today, staring into one of these, I realized that it looked a little better. This isn't good. How ugly has the world become wherein commercial art has ,after what, like half a decade of completely fitting in, now stood out?

A chilling period to enter.

DIVISION OF NEIGHBOR

There's a girl ordering her drink at the counter and she's wearing a Crystal Castles shirt. I love that band, and I'm almost certain she's attractive. This means nothing though. I see an Alexandria Cortez patch on the military bag slung on her shoulder.

My generation has no Vietnam. Instead, we have a million individual daily wars, usually of little to no meaning. Today's war starts here with me realizing that although I could briefly listen to this girl's boring female empowerment drivel, she could never give my thoughts that same light of day. There is no reciprocation, and that's fine. We'd get along until she figured out that I don't believe in the moon landing or the heliocentric model. But the issue stems deeper than just this. The bands her and I both love lean towards her side of the political spectrum. They want open borders. They want racists and sexists dead. They want everyone to know that our government is staffed with Ku-Klux-Klan wizards, a group that has been comprised almost exclusively of federal agents since it was restarted. There is no place in civil discussion for these kinds of people. Civil discussion is gay, anyways. That's why sitting on our hands is pointless. These people need to be dragged out into the streets and shot before they do exactly that to us.

A large majority of obscure artistic culture is dominated by left-wing radicals. I'm not sure that you could even call them that. These people are politically impotent and religiously atheist, subscribing to whatever is most popular at the moment. They dedicate themselves to some brain-dead cause and the result of this useless struggle is the latest, greatest experimental-indie album. They pour hours into an instrument thinking about how the proceeds will go to displaced African refugees when, in reality, the profit margin gets soaked up by super-global mega-corps. These are without question the worst revolutionaries time has ever seen. Kill someone important! Burn something down! Cut yourself for attention! Anything! The gas pedal is waiting to be stepped on. It never is though. At least not by these losers.

Regardless of all their faults, I still find between us just a sliver of common ground. They do not, and so this is where discourse ends. I realize they have the right idea, about just hating anyone who doesn't mostly agree with you, and I hate back once more. This can't go on forever. It won't. This standoff can only end in violence. Weaklings of their caliber do not survive in the outside world.

Café girl finishes her order and when she turns around I smile. She smiles back. It's in this moment that I feel what just a fraction of her affection is like. I could have it all if I lied about what I think. I'm certainly handsome enough, out of her league even. A word or two later and I could be a 'fascist' with a bloody nose and chai tea all over my tailored vintage flannel. Her teeth would look good on a curb.

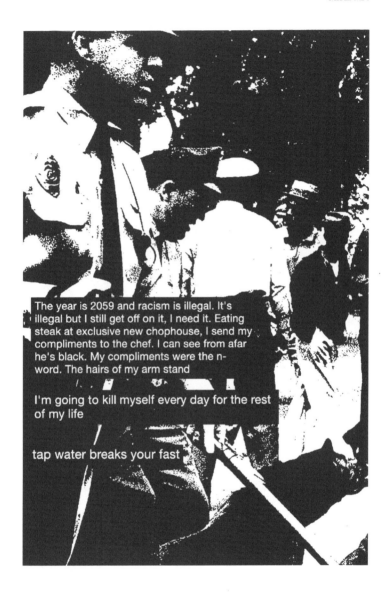

The year is 2059 and racism is illegal. It's illegal but I still get off on it, I need it. Eating steak at exclusive new chophouse, I send my compliments to the chef. I can see from afar he's black. My compliments were the n-word. The hairs of my arm stand

I'm going to kill myself every day for the rest of my life

tap water breaks your fast

AT THE DRIVE THROUGH

Oh, I'm sure you've heard it so many times, but the truth of the matter is this: Not only is everyone starring in that movie inside their heads, but the movies and other inspirations behind it all continues to get worse. Maybe there was a time when the people based their personal mental movie on things of better taste and, in effect, this made them slightly better to be around. But now, at this late or otherwise stage in the lowerworld, the characters have all become so lame. It ranges from bad to worse, from the people who parrot Disney Channel conversation fragments to the faggots firing off Reddit lingo and dork-film mannerisms, from worse to horrible. Frat-flick mimickers, reality television nightmare sluts, action film philosophers, the drooling masses who dream of their sci-fi superhero of the galaxy moment. I understand their need for synthetic 'motivation', that tiny artificial something to help them mold a sort of identity, but what we see now is just plain bad. I wish I could say that people were playing out bastardized versions of their favorite ultra-wild superhero movie characters, but we don't even get that.

No wage-slave New Yorker dressing up in tights and savagely beating black drug dealers after sunset. No hyper-dyke midwestern outcast running churchgoers over with stolen truck painted neon pink. No super-rapist who rapes other rapists. The closest thing we have to movie super heroes is school shooters, maybe. In reality, these other people get their fill of "AHHH I'M IN THE MOVIES, BUT IN MY HEAD… AND I DID SUCH AN AWESOME THING" by simply ordering Marvel merchandise and reusing said movie's humor until a graceless death. The kind of death that in any other time would be mistaken for a triple-decade suicide.

The people you walk by every day are computer generated images. They are digitized fill-ins, computer bodies delivering lines to fill the empty space. Where there's a gap, there may be a guy in superhero fan gear. Where there's some room, you could find a sassy black college girl and her gay Latin friend with green hair. Maybe you yourself are generated by computers to fill the void.

What exactly is being shot, you ask? It's untitled for now. The movie is shit — too long, too lacking. The main characters are all dead and have been for the past five decades – although some believe it's more like two centuries. Where it stands now is poorly. Consider the whole project a three-legged stool where two have been kicked out at once. Consider the whole project a once-good something that lost nearly all that kept it beautiful. Consider that at one point in the film, only a half per cent of the project, it all fell apart. Here we are, still recording.

Nothing makes sense anymore because it doesn't follow the blueprint. No direction, no end in sight — everything is wild and silly! Women with fingers that fit inside keyholes but never unlock very much. Pain that sears human skin like thick steaks on high heat. Weather machines that reopen and stitch shut our wounds intermittently, all because machines can speak to one another. Boys and girls, men and women. Someone telling you to hold hands with the people you hate, forever. A film that once walked and somewhere along the line stepped into a voidhole. A manmade pit to catch all possibility.

Yeah, you are in that movie in your head, but it fucking sucks and it'll never end. We're all here. The casting director blew it. There is no walking away from the explosion scene. There is no tear-jerking redemption scene. There is no 'all was lost but now it is found' scene. There isn't even an end — the director probably left.

Yeah, yeah. Even this book is some kind of role-play, isn't it? Who am I channeling? What scene or character or movie am I stealing this entire brand of literature from? What personality traits am I lifting? What am I correctly failing to articulate, or articulating just right? What is my role-play most closely sourced from? What could I be doing better? Who do I think I'm akin to?

If I wrote it all in sonnets, it'd be taking from him.
If I wrote it all in free-form poetry, it'd be a little too close to her.
If I sang it from a window in Paris, someone would call me a faggot.

We are however far into this world and you are asking me not to take a little from here or use a little from that? At this point, the building blocks look a lot like the other building blocks beneath them, and those before them resemble some others until forever. Maybe I'll read the entire Western Canon to ensure that my every word is the first in print. Maybe I'll invent a new language and say crazy things nobody ever has. Maybe I'll just keep absorbing new particles from this and unloading into the ancient template from that.

If I wrote it all in a magazine, it's really kind of this man.
If I wrote it all on parchment, it's reminiscent of that dear sir.
If I said it all to groups of people along the way, Pontius would hang me up to dry.

People say "damned if you do, damned if you don't" about a fair share of things. It makes a kind of larger sense here. You'll always have nails driven through your hands and feet. You'll always wear the crown of thorns. You'll always get made fun of by someone on the internet.

To some words are currency, investments. Who knows.

A TORTURE WITHOUT PAIN

A room inside the ocean at night. A ceiling just above its surface. It is pitch black aside from a single sea-green light on the bow of an old and creaking wood ship. It howls every time the waves shift it. You're laying twenty feet ahead of it, affixed to a bed that moves also with the waves. Below you is the ravenous sea, dark as anything could become. No explanation, no method of escape, nothing. This is how you woke up one day. And it's how you remain forever.

LA CRETURA

The people of now are what can only be called creatures or demons. These people are not people. Some will say their look is normal, that it's the result of a lifelong lived, of the regular burdens — they are wrong. Normal burdens and days of honest work do not make people into what you'll find walking around here. "Here" is everywhere, but primarily America. Is America the vehicle through which Satan enters the world? Myself and many others are hard-pressed to disprove it.

AR WAR E

There's a thought that constantly crosses my mind and it's that we've all become too self-aware. And then I think about it some more and I say to myself, "maybe that isn't so true."

I don't know what to believe anymore. There are days where I feel like I've hyper-analyzed every detail of every individual moment and the next coming event is my introduction to the creator of the maybe-simulation built around and inside of me.

There's a 'striking amount of people who don't understand the science behind thick girls. Fat is fat, we know this. But thick falls within very fine lines. It's a product of pure nature, a glimpse of Eden, the sacrosanct in symphony. When all is in order, the connoisseur could weep.

"Thick ends where fat begins," I whisper into my lap.

I, and many others, have sexualized it too much – there's now a market for borderline fat women and, in my conquest for the revival of feminine figure, I've contributed to its downfall. This is my own fault. Most of the time I'm just tired of seeing too much hipbone on a woman.

Did you know the CIA put anime into black communities nationwide? Undoubtedly of their strangest psychological operations to date, followed by the introduction of crack-cocaine and World Star Hip Hop. All of these factors combined leaves us with what we see today. Fatherless black males, dressed in Naruto costumes, stealing and destroying things in various chain stores and fast food locations. Yes, this is a form of acceleration.

HONEST WORK DOESN'T WORK.

What'll it be? How will you ride this life out? Do you work in what you consider to be an honest trade, five days a week for the rest of your life, maybe more and maybe less? Do you scam and grift and steal everything from a world you see as rotten regardless?

What is honest work anymore? Seven months to build a department store. Seven months of work — electricians, masons, framers, plumbers, realtors, painters, floorers, upper management. Seven months after completion, it closes, because nobody fucking cares about a chain store when the internet has everything and cheaper. Seven months alongside creatures who snuck over the border wall to work for wages so low that even the "good old American" types will subcontract them. There's a superintendent walking around with the country's flag on his shoulder, watching illegal aliens misalign studs and door frames — he says nothing to object. You'd get fired if you ripped that flag off his reflective jacket. He doesn't care; he finds new ways to shift the blame. He acts like it's someone else's job to smash the windows out of the invasive creature vehicles. Honest work, is it? The result is a department store that you were forced to build with your enemies. It closes down and you do it again a couple months later. We should be building gargantuan monuments, statues, temples that look good inside and out. We should be building alongside people who belong here, who look like we do. You and I were scammed. You were scammed. I was scammed. But it is on us to reverse the heavy damages. It is on us to burn it all down.

What is honest work? Selling poisonous food to already poisoned people? Selling useless shit to the useful idiots? Selling things to people that then sell those things too? In this moment, the noblest trade is mastering the art of leisure. I can't think of a smarter person than someone who figures how to rob the system blind and never work again. I can't think of a smarter person than someone who successfully leeches off government programs. With good taste of course. The best of all trade work is aristocracy. Our working class is completely dead inside; anyone who has spent a day's time around them can attest to this. This "honest work" — building dollar stores, mall temples, ratholes — it takes hostage the soul of many could-be heroes. If "honest work" was human, he'd be charged with many crimes, one of which against nature. God sits above and mourns the construction of yet another strip mall. It's true. I've seen and felt him do so. God to me sometimes feels like a close and personal friend and he looks often disappointed, even in me. He mourns the destruction of his lush and hungry forests for game store number seven-thousand and Chinese buffet number whatever.

Those responsible for decisions like these will pay dearly for this level of sin; you'd have to be a fucking idiot to think you escape free of punishment.

All this "honest work" kills the beauty and creativity in man. It forces men into poor diet, poor choices, poor paths outside the workplace. Everything in life for them, whether they chose so or not, must revolve around their job. No time to research, shop for, and cook a proper meal so he has chips and soda again. No time to work out, to worship the sun in peace, to study old books, so he watches television and jerks off in-between beers again. No time to even consider another way of life so he hammers nails into useless shit in a useless place again. You are being scammed, robbed.

It's a sin to drown yourself in work forever, unless of course that work produces things of greatness. Chances are that's not the case. We used to build massive holy temples with ancient machinery running on free energy. Now we build sporting good stores.

Quit your job and rob the world blind, legally if you can manage it. Honest work here today, in this lower kind of world, is a spook. Complete illusion. You aren't a better person for making money in a "respectable" fashion — you are handicapped and lying to yourself. Honest work is a confused and pointless shot in the foot. You'll limp home every day for the rest of your life. Quit your job and sit in the sun every day. Quit your job and run away into the woods forever. Quit your job and shoot a politician. Escape by speedboat off the coast of Miami, hide in the tropics somewhere. Do it again there, speedboat even farther south. Kill your miser boss and his miser boss and escape using one of their private jets. Go to the marina at night with twenty-five friends and steal every yacht you can. Sail as a fleet, down into the southern world, and conquer small towns. Kill yourself if it doesn't work out. Fly to the Middle East, build a harem of Arab women, and declare war on the

United States with your new rebel army. Or just keep making department stores until you rot away, maybe have a couple beers and play a little golf in-between.

Do you understand how many arsonists go uncaught? Not even close to caught? Just figure out how to do it and start soon. Start burning ugly shit down. To be working class in this day and age is to be suicidal and complacent. Or maybe you just don't get it.

NAP THAT FEELS LIKE FEVER DREAM

There's too much going on inside my head. I'm not panicked or visibly upset. Not ever and especially not now. I don't think I've ever been nervous in my life. Still, there's still too much going on inside my head.

I cannot stop thinking about how much I do not know. I cannot stop thinking about how drastically rearranged tomorrow would be if I read a certain sentence today. Tomorrow could end with my mother prying at the hands of the police escorting me to a cruiser in handcuffs. If I said the right combination of words to a beautiful girl, she'd lay her head on my chest that night. If I thought deeply and connected the right pieces I could have government officials hanged for treason in a public courtyard. If I didn't have anything inside my head at all, maybe I could finally sleep. I want to know how many butterflies fly within the effect.

Something happens and the slate wipes clean; I fall tenderly into daydream.

My arms are resting underneath my head, supporting it above the pillow. The shades are pulled halfway and the afternoon sunlight compliments my torso with some alternating stripes. I stay like this for a little bit. It's nice and I can forget about everything. It doesn't last, though. I'm still in the daydream but something shifts. That blank canvas of two minutes ago is being spun around and paraded on. I think about what would happen if I actually took my own life. I think about it a lot, in a serious fashion, but within safe limits. If I wanted to die, I'd have done it already.

I think about whether or not I've become too pretentious. I don't care, I've mentally routed this all before.

i think about how writing in only lowercase would lure a new demographic into reading this book. hello sophia from new york city. i see you as you open at random to specifically this page, by total coincidence. it's not coincidence, in reality. i wanted you here, in this obscure manhattan book shop that you kill time in until your friend says she's outside. tonight, when you walk home, ill follow you and catch the main door to your apartment complex before it closes (don't want to ask a stranger for the code). ill watch you undress only to stare disgusted at yourself in the $10 walmart mirror your parents had shipped to you, at your request. you couldn't afford that? really? ill watch you order takeout time and time again because you are far too "busy" to learn how to cook your own meals. sophia, ill watch you cry over shitty netflix shows. ill watch you molest yourself to porn you found thru extremely SPECIFIC search terms. ill watch you spend more of your parents money on things in poor taste. you were stuck for a while, debating whether or not you could pull off fake designer or not. i saw that. you went with the real one, surprisingly. not really surprising, it's your parents money. ill watch you attempt a new workout routine, which lasts all of

exactly 5 minutes. ill watch you lose a little more ambition. ill watch you read listicles on buzzfeed, the ones you share with your friends who don't actually click them when you send it. you keep doing this for months and come summer they will lose all respect for you. especially elizabeth — she's not a total normie like you and she's well aware that buzzfeed is for empty fuckups like you, sophia. ill watch you for all this time and not once lust for you, SOPHIA. SOPHIA YOU DISGUST ME AND YOUR PARENTS ALIKE. SOPHIA, STOP GETTING DRUNK AND VENTING TO BODEGA CLERKS. THE ONE YOU'VE BEEN FREQUENTING AS OF LATE CAN'T EVEN SPEAK ENGLISH. HE MASTURBATES TO YOU WHEN HE GETS HOME. SOMETIMES HE CAN'T EVEN WAIT THAT LONG AND HE'LL CAUTIOUSLY START RIGHT THERE, UNDER THE REGISTER, WHEN HE THINKS NOBODY IS AROUND. SOPHIA, YOU'RE GONNA GET RAPED AGAIN IF YOU KEEP DRINKING LIKE YOU DO IN THE PLACES YOU GO.

SOPHIA, THOSE "CUTE, WELL-READ, PRO-FEMALE" NYU GUYS BUY THEIR ROOFIES THE SAME WAY EVERYONE ELSE DOES: WITH WADDED AND SWEATY CASH, GIDDILY, HALF-ERECT AT THE THOUGHT OF THE NIGHT AHEAD. IN THE HOURS LEADING UP TO SAID NIGHT, THEY'LL STARE INTO THE PILL LIKE A MAGIC EIGHT BALL. "WILL I GET LUCKY TONIGHT?" HE SAYS, SHAKING IT AROUND IN THE BAG. IT SETTLES AND READS "YES, GRANTED THE BATHROOM DOOR HAS A LOCK AND THE MUSIC IS LOUD". SOPHIA, YOU SAD SOW — YOU BROUGHT THIS ON YOURSELF. SOPHIA YOU RAPED THE WORLD WITH BAD DECISIONS AND

NOW IT RAPES YOU BACK. HOW MANY TIMES WILL YOU EXCUSE A MESSY DRUNKEN NIGHT WITH JESUS' DYING ON THE CROSS. THAT WASN'T FOR YOUR SINS. YOUR SINS ARE YOURS, AND YOURS ALONE. YOUR SINS ARE YOURS TO CARRY.

YOU KNOW THOSE PEOPLE WHO SPEND ALL DAY SHIT-TALKING RELIGIOUS FAITH ON REDDIT? JESUS DIED FOR THEIR SINS, EVEN, BUT NOT YOURS. HOW PATHETIC, SOPHIA. HE DIED FOR MINE, SOPHIA. DO YOU WANNA SEE HOW I'VE SINNED LATELY? SOPHIA, YOU BROUGHT THIS ON YOURSELF, SOPHIA THE SAD SOW. SAD, SAD, PATHETIC AND SAD. SOPHIA, FIX THIS. SOPHIA, ONLY A PACT WITH SATAN CAN SAVE YOU NOW. SOPHIA, SOPHIA, SOPHIA. STOP READING BUZZFEED SOPHIA STOP NOW. STOP SHARING THEIR LISTS. STOP DRINKING BAREFOOT WINE ALONE. STOP DRINKING SUTTER HOME ALONE.

BUY A GUN SOPHIA. POINT IT AT YOUR HEAD WHEN YOU ARE SAD, HALF-JOKINGLY, HALF-SERIOUS. IT'S USUALLY UNLOADED AND THE DRY FIRE CLICK MAKES YOU FEEL GOOD BUT THIS MORNING I BROKE INTO YOUR APARTMENT AND PUT A LIVE ROUND IN THE CHAMBER. TONIGHT, AFTER YOU GET WINE-DRUNK YET AGAIN, YOU'LL PICK IT UP AND SCARE YOUR GAY NEIGHBORS. WHAT A WAY TO GO. COMMITTING SUICIDE BY ACCIDENT BUT NOBODY EVER KNOWS THAT. THEY WILL ALWAYS THINK YOU WANTED OUT, REALLY REALLY BAD. L O L .

I think about what everyone defines as love. A lot of people always say it's about forgetting the things you dislike in a person. That's stupid. I could adapt to anything and so could million other people. That feeling of a daydream's shift comes once again and I forget what I think love is.

A few days ago there would have been a girl lying beside me during this break. She'd coil up in my arms with hair smelling of expensive shampoo. I'd be worrying that we wasted the day inside when we could have gone fishing or hiking or swimming at a lake that nobody really talks about. I would resolve this worry by mentally noting that tonight we could get some fancy dinner. That would repair any lazy decisions of the day, for me at least. A few days ago, she would smile when I told her this resolution. She would say okay with an excited tone, half-awake, tugging on the base of my collar, and then fall back asleep. A few days ago, I would hunt for a decent place to take her and quietly make our reservations. I'd slip back into bed, carefully navigating the tangled arms and never wake her up. Maybe she tosses around a little bit, but she stays within her dreams.

For someone who argues for the tasteful abuse of women, I am a kind soul. There is no sense in hating them, at least not all of them. Some deserve Hellfire, and some can be used to your advantage. With one eye open, they might even be lovable. I have nothing but respect for the opposing gender. Opposite gender.

EAGLES DESCENDING UPON CAPISTRANO WITH TONGUES LIKE WILTED FLOWERS, FOREVER.

I aim to construct for you a vision of the world that makes clear one thing: God cannot be reached, nor can he reach us, so long as we surround ourselves in the unchecked technological expansion. From just around the industrial revolution forward, God has been rapidly phased out by the fruits of ill labor. It only gets worse every day. Another cell tower erected is another spot in which God becomes blind. At this point, with the amount we've built, it is safely assumed that He's unable to see our world at all. Not to mention the number of other monstrosities that disrupt the once existent state of harmony. Heaven's Light is snubbed by shields of internetwork, bluetooth connections, and phone link entanglements. We've boxed God out, given ourselves strange cancers and illnesses, and become dependent on something historically and extremely undependable, unknown — this is the absolute state of today. It burns to exist now because simply existing here is sinful enough.

It's worth wondering if sin even carries the same weight anymore. Are nefarious actions against a demonic and upside-down world still punishable? And if so, are they punished a little less?

The way I see it, sins are only sins when unleashed upon a world that doesn't deserve it — a world that you don't want to see hurt — better known as the previous world. To have disgraced the world when it was at its most beautiful was worthy of ample Helltime. But now, when the world is so ugly and itself unclean, how can you consider action against it as sin? I would go as far to claim that any action meant to collapse this place sooner, effectively making way for new life, would be considered holy — maybe even ordainable by a kind of state-aware papacy.

I don't mean to speak for God, but one must seriously wonder these things. When you've been starved so long of his contact, of any sign that he's still holding the mighty ship's wheel, you grow radicalized. But not always against Him. What do you do when even the places of worship have become so bastardized and weak? Where do you congregate? Where do you confess? Where do you repent? Where do you devote yourself to a life of allegiance to above? Where do you go to accept God into your heart when so many have commercialized and uglified the act of doing so? I don't want to be handed a Gildan heavy cotton church group tee shirt as a welcome for becoming one with Christ. I want to be welcomed by surroundings that feel as pure as the Earth itself always does. I want there to be a connection between the creation and creator in the place that claims to know Him. I want to see the ugly burned out forever because it's an affront, plain and simple.

It's hard to care beyond this all. I don't want to depend on the higher world. Nobody should fully depend on it. Maybe it's there for minor guidance or maybe God only helps those who help themselves. Perhaps He isn't even there. Perhaps the Watchers never broke through the firmament. It could be that the higher world is only the clouds that rain down every so often. Either way, I roam.

MIDNIGHT SNACK, HOMESHAKE

Following their last monumental album, *In The Shower*, Homeshake creates yet another work of greatness. I'm iffy about even calling them albums, as each song blends so effortlessly into the next. Appropriately titled *Midnight Snack*, the pieces on this record are distinctly about having sex. It all begins with an introduction called *What Did He Look Like*, an acid-trip phone call over leather guitar and simple drums. This carries into *Heat*, an early contender for the album's best track.

"All alone and got nothing to do, except to lie awake and dream of you."

The song sets beautifully the tone of the album, establishing a necessary sexual tension to be broken, something shattered perfectly across the record later on. It's about planning the act with your lover. At least this is what I took away from it.

"She talks to me about heat."

Next comes *He's Heating Up!,* a far-from-ambiguous track about the ritualism behind the approaching nightcap. Peter Sagar, the lead of Homeshake, also discusses here the presence of another man trying to interrupt the process.

I Don't Wanna is the album's sudden shift. Following a record scratch, the track tackles the idea that maybe this wasn't such a good idea. You're left wondering if one of the participants isn't so keen anymore… but there's a whole album ahead of them. The show must go on. All is set to return to good spirits, but doesn't. *Faded* gives us a small glimmer of hope. The two are still together, likely stoned and questioning the world, but together in that. Is it enough?

"Baby I don't know what to do. Look at us, it's just me and you."

We can live with this knowledge, as its progress towards the bigger picture. Such a strong start means only great things, we like to think.

Love Is Only A Feeling begins with a sharp, Princian synth met at the break with classic Homeshake style jam-jazz. It's almost pretty enough to distract the listener from the further demise of the protagonist's journey. Like anger, pity, and disgust, he now believes that love is only another feeling.

A bright, boisterous keyboard pulls us from the gutter. A

single synth and only that under the voices of *Under the Sheets*. This is the glimpse of hope we so eagerly waited for in the past three songs. The night will commence and he's confident that this girl loves him. What more could we ask for?

Real Love is a soulful testament to the night's return. He's in the club, packed tight with women he could care nothing less about. And just like that, he sees her there. They lock eyes and take a breath. It's real love. He knows this now.

The album is back in full swing with *Move This Body* as our protagonist fights his way through the crowd, sweaty and tight knit. He's making his way to her to ask one thing,

"Hey baby, you wanna come dance with me?"

She takes his hand. He feels nervous — because moving is what she plans to do.

NOT ENOUGH VIOLENCE

The difference between good and bad criminals depends on how well they were dressed. It depends on what weapon they used. It depends on their posture, their voice, their plan of attack. It depends on how they carried themselves. It depends on how they carried it out. It depends on their height, their frame, their bone structure, their body fat percentage, their haircut. It depends on who their victim was. Even the very worst of criminal acts are forgiven by simply looking good. Or cool. Or interesting, in some way.

This is why droves of people idolize certain criminals. The Columbine shooters, the LA Shootout gunmen, Dylann Roof, Elliot Rodger, Omar Mateen, Ted Kaczynski, Killdozer, and so on. This is also why some get left behind, only remembered for the amount they killed or their embarrassing backstory, like the

Parkland shooter, the Las Vegas shooter, Virginia Tech, etc. Of course, the whole fascination isn't purely aesthetic-focused. Today's population will generally love anything or anyone that causes massive societal disruption. The people love a good disturbance. Agency-funded or not.

ISIS understands this well, for the most part. A black flag, white letters in the center.

"There is no god but Allah."

Even in the Arabic scribble they use, it pleases the eye. But further than that, it's intimidating beyond belief. It's mounted on the tanks and armed trucks that storm into Middle Eastern towns with raw force; those six words in white let know the people what's coming – shameless acts of ultra-violence filmed in crystal clear high-definition, uploaded for the masses to witness. Executions portrayed so vividly that the first-world can feel nerves splitting too. It's suspiciously cinematic.

The uniforms don't fall far from the tree. Fitted and sometimes tailored assortments of digital and desert camo, juxtaposed with black cloth and face covers to match. Ski masks, combat boots, AK-47s, bandoliers of extra magazines slung over the chest. With even minimal taste and maximal attitude comes pending influence. They capture not just cities, but hearts and minds. Mothers, children, teens, fighting-age males, you name it. Raqqa falls to ISIS at night and by morning, droves of new allies fall into line. They understand the importance of fashionable terror. They may also be a little scared. As I'm sure you've heard before, it's "hearts and minds, because physical wounds heal."

Of course, I'm not justifying the acts of the Islamic State, only mentioning how a group of rebels and misfits made it so far within a mess of Middle Eastern conflicts. Fleets of Toyota Tacoma's with mounted machine guns jimmy-rigged into the truck beds tends to grant you a little power. Selling gargantuan amounts of oil to your handler-state of Israel also helps.

Violence without good story or style is barbaric at best. You can get away with a lot if you look a little better. Maximize looks to maximize crime, and in that, accelerate better. Consider it crimemaxing. Next time you are thinking about robbing an armored truck, put a little time and money into the outfit you'll be wearing. When the urge to smash every windshield of every car at your local dealership strikes, tone up beforehand. Pick some nice boots, a nice mask, chin up and shoulders back. This is going to be on the news tomorrow.

TURN BACK NOW OR FOREVER GO ON$_x$

Walking past government casino. See flock of sickos dancing around outside. Talks of they won this, he won that, she won more. All in golf clothes. A bunch of gopher-toothed golf sluts. Golf monkeys. Outfits handpicked from the sporting goods shop. I am a conduit of punishment. Wire runs through me, live and dangerous, and it burns federal stoppers like sun-dry paper. I channel high voltage. When they grab onto me, when they complete my circuit, it blows holes in their bodies. It blows their arms off, blows out the tips of their elbows, out their everythings. You might forget reality but it's all there. I don't trip when I short. I'm a bomb that pops forever. A ghost that haunts the longest.

PHONE CALL WITH A FRIEND

My friend calls me and he's drunk.

"Should I start doing steroids? I want to get stronger so I can beat my girlfriend. Not that I couldn't already, I just want to beat the shit out of her even harder."

I laugh and hang up. I know he's too drunk to even realize we were speaking.

MONDAY'S WAR

Man was once the sum of his choices, maybe the books he read, or the people he spoke with. Today, man is the sum of that all in addition to the videos he's seen, the number of people who like him online, the amount of government-sanctioned foodpoison he's consumed, and so much more. You are now, from the start, the death you will become – unless of course you defer to our holy originators. Life's most violent pain is the result of nature denied. It is the careful blueprint contractors often ignore, nature. They think they know more than it has to offer. They think they know how to operate outside its ways. But it will forever and always win. Submission to nature is one of the only submissions you should welcome in life.

It's Monday morning and I have been cleaning the house to loud music. Compulsively. I take off my clothes and jump into some workout stuff. Olive green shorts, maybe a shirt, maybe not. Def Leppard playing at full volume. As a warmup, I'll do twenty handcuffs, followed by Y's/T's/W's/and I's. These being the arm stretches, of course. When I'm good and warm I'll start lifting weights. Every day is a bench press day, for the most part. Often times it's incline, but sometimes it's flat bench. Sometimes the reverse. I'll switch grips and approaches to keep things fresh, to give the muscles some form of rest. Sometimes overhead press for months on end, sometimes only once a week. It's all dependent on how I feel right then and there. This is liquid weight lifting.

There are days where I don't feel like counting the reps anymore. Routine is great, but I like to venture out sometimes. In between sets I will box the air and scream until I'm covered in sweat. I'll turn the air conditioning off for a little extra fire. More screaming. Screaming until I can see the neighbors crowded at the edge of my lawn, discussing my screaming. Sometimes the cops knock and make sure everything is okay. Never talk to cops. Additionally, I don't stop moving until the levee breaks at my eyebrows and sweat bites my eyes. I want to squint and see an overworked body shine in the morning sunlight. I want to know I've done something today because it'll eat away at me later on if I don't. I want to be angry and red-faced in the plank position until it hurts. I always want a better body. Something, something about there being no right to be out of shape, something, something Socrates.

To be strong is to be on the right side of history.

Physical fitness is inherently correct. It's always in style, timeless and waiting. All the things required of someone to be truly in shape are all things scumbags not only despise, but despise out of inability. Inner strength, outer strength, courage, self-control, a desire to sweat and bleed for results. Your standard worm-brain faggot would rather stay weak than submit to the fascist creation known as the gym. Strength is imposing and bold, so yes, strength is fascism — I guess maybe they are right about that. When you see disgusting pigs like ██████████████ or ████████████ just remember, they've shown you their hand of cards. Don't be surprised when they beg you to meet the enemy half way. Act accordingly against the yeastern kind, the weak, the unwilling. Make them submit. They must submit.

I shower and it's tough to raise my arms over my head. My muscles are torn and they will rebuild even bigger than before. I get out, dry off, part my hair, brush my teeth, et cetera.

I put on my boxers, my pants, my socks. I throw on a Ralph Lauren flannel to spite the early-approaching summer. I put on my shoes which always used to be beige sneakers but are now always western boots in some kind of light desert color. Maybe it's time for sneakers again. Then I put on my insecurities. Now I'm leaving for the store. I need butcher shop meats. Game meats. Raw milk. Sauerkraut. Kefir. Gallons of blood. Considering getting some oats as well, but probably won't. Oats register to me as an anti-nutrient these days. Your body whispers to you these secrets if you only stop and listen.

In the car I listen to Death In June's best album, *But, What Ends When The Symbols Shatter?*.

After I get what I needed and head back to refrigerate it, I decide to stop by my favorite thrift store and get some books. This is my favorite thing to do here in town. The books are fifty cents each, a total steal. My goal is to fill my house, wall to wall, with any worthwhile literature I find there. I'm still not sure if I ever learned to read.

I'm home now, sitting beside the stack of books I found today. Four dollars and happy with it. Moments like these, humble as they are, confirm my stepping away from the tailspinning void. I'm eating raw beef liver in triple doses. I'm taking sunlight in like I need it to live, because I do.

Still, at times, that apathetic claw reaches from that apathetic dark. It calls out something like:

"Come with me, or don't."

I try to understand life from the void. I embrace it with caution, one foot still inside the light. I look over the shoulder of whomever the claw belongs to and see a dozen similar figures in the shadows.

"If you guys don't care, why don't you just die," I shout.

"Too much work," they all reply now — in unison.

"And what happens if you succeed? What happens if you pull us all down there?" I continue. I'm likely veiny in the face from screaming and using too many hand motions.

"Whatever happens, does."

I wish I could genuinely believe that God had existed and then died in this very world. I don't really wish that. Though God's death would explain all the decay, all the twisted parts and pieces. Suddenly, it's easier to swallow. Maybe, just maybe, we could all sleep at night knowing that child sex rings, false flag operations, rampant abortion, and never finding love were neatly penciled into the docket. Maybe we could sleep at night if together we understood that God wasn't around to stop the bad guys anymore. In his absence, evil gained a strong footing. Oh well. In that case, with a matter so unreachably high and divine, man couldn't be at blame. How can he fix what he isn't capable of fixing?

Long after he's gone, long after the bloated corpse of God has decayed in full, the angels protecting the Gates of Heaven will abandon post to watch our mortal world in retrograde. Everything burns and nothing seems so bad. It doesn't feel good either, because it just kind of is. What is the death of beauty to those who never saw it? Monday. And what is the erasure of human life to those who never valued it? Less traffic tomorrow morning.

The fires will rage for years and not once will someone think to put them out. At the end of it all, we sit in a big circle and let the clothes singe off our backs; the skin melts down the bones and the bones crumble into ash soon after. "Planet Earth, have you heard of it? They were a strange kind," the onlookers will say from nearby places. Places we never got to explore because ours came crashing down. And we'd be lying to say we cared.

A nihilist is most easily defeated by his next utility bill.

"I could tell a joke and make the whole room laugh, but I don't bother. No, I don't bother."

TUESDAY NIGHT'S DEATH SENSOR

I'm in trouble. An old friend, a girl, invited me over for drinks and I went. I don't drink and she did, a lot. Next thing I know I'm tipping a full bookcase onto her and she's completely broken underneath it. A justified self-defense scenario.

Have you ever seen someone die from pain rather than right away? They writhe with the most terrifying facial expression. It's like they are panic frozen. It looks similar to when you bunch up a straw wrapper and place a single droplet of water on it. I wish I could describe it better, but I can't, so you'll either have to find out for yourself or move on.

The bookcase snapped perfectly down the center, vertically, and fragments of the cheap IKEA "wood" lacerated head to toe. She's not even crying because the broken ribcage simply won't allow for it. I squat down, adjusting the legs of my pants, to look into her eyes. I'm not laughing yet but I can feel it building just behind my teeth. Then something makes me crack. I'm cackling, then giggling, then sighing once I realize I'm alone in doing so. I pace and pause.

"Right, anyways…" I tap the bookcase twice and go out the back door towards my car.

In the car, I think about something – life is just a constant remembering and forgetting negative things. Positive too. It is also about hunting and eating animals with your bare hands. And being in the sun. worshipping the sun.

You're outside, standing under the sun at the hottest it'll ever burn today, and the world shifts to catch your stride. Something about the way you breathe has you feeling fluid, and it's common to you now. You walk barefoot and it doesn't hurt. You decide you might take down a tree with an axe of your making. You might burn the center out and drift into another place. Canoe and axe alone, you're learning how to chain the living momentum together. After a while, you don't need anything from anyone. You don't need advice. You don't need attention. You don't need care. You're killing and catching, growing to harvest, putting smiles on the faces of elder blood. Everything ancient is within you, not class is taught about it.

WEDNESDAY

While checking out this job site, a car dealership, I overhear the superintendent talking with some desk jockey about how the homeless keep breaking in and stealing material every night. Locks, cameras, security guards — nothing works. They come in huge numbers from the woods just nearby. It's a giant encampment of probably fifty or more homeless people. They've got a stockpile of weapons and cars, even a couple crackwhores they send out as scouts during daylight. The police refuse to intervene as it's "way too dangerous". I wait until the conversation tapers off, til the desk guy heads out.

"Listen," I tell the super, pulling him into a security camera blind spot, "there's no other way around this problem besides the one solution I'm sure has more than crossed your mind. You need some people to go in there and quietly wipe that camp out. That's your only way out, man."

He laughs, nervously, and accuses me of reading his mind.

"Is it dramatic? Yeah, a little," I concede. "But it has to be done. The insurance guys aren't going to keep paying out."

We go outside and discuss a little more, plan to meet at a later time in a less-watched place. What a world.

THURSDAY FINALLY_x

"When you are with women, you are alone. When you are with homosexuals, you are alone. When you are with men far outside your socioeconomic class, you are alone. You will, for the majority of your life, be alone," a friend tells me.

Some people are lucky enough to find like-minded men of similar status. Those are the men that you stand by for life.

FRIDAY AND I'M BREATHING
COLD AIR LIKE SOME KIND OF DRUG

The days become a blur during this absolute spiraling nose dive of a week. Maybe it's been two weeks. I care about things but it probably doesn't seem so. There's something I'm not noticing, something I haven't pieced together. It may be something I have yet to cut out. I'm considering an elimination diet except for everything in my entire life.

We can't continue consuming the eye, mind, food, and water poisons of this present world. It cannot keep happening like this. It really cannot keep happening like this. There's a way out, something easy or not, that cures us of this all. The cure may not be of our choosing, it may be forced upon us. Much like how Native Americans believe the colonists were cursed for building on ancient burial grounds, I believe the entire modern world is cursed for not only building over the bones of time since past, but in a terrible way. There's a curse upon the present for not putting something better in place of the past. I won't whine to you about what monstrosities replaced what was once beautiful, what is now a fast food place instead of something else. Just know why bad things happen to us now. You must understand this. It is an explanation strong enough to displace others such as the death of God, or his not ever existing.

The only way to acquire pure water now is by collecting rain on Sunday. During his only day of rest, the Lord weeps unto us.

GYM SHARKS

Women never get home gyms because then nobody would give them the attention they want. The rare few who do build home gyms will proceed to upload squat videos to Instagram. If you can imagine it, they will always squat in the tightest pants they own — never a slightly loose pair of sweatpants, never a burka.

THE TIMES, A BAR

I show up to the bar and my friends are nowhere to be found. Probably at the rooftop area if I had to guess. I climb the stairs and see them towards the far corner.

"Hey, there he is!" an unrecognizable face calls out.

I'm not wearing my glasses and I don't know these people well enough to distinguish them in my blindness. I near closer and all is well, it's "Dillon".

I shake everyone's hand and sit on a stool among the group.

The conversation shifts rapidly, coerced by the drunken eagerness of people who read too much Huffington Post. I'm struggling to keep up and I'm entirely sober.

I catch a break in the heat of debate and interject with a classic rambling that will inevitably end in dirty looks. They are discussing the surge of transgender and non-binary people coming out with pride, saying it's a beautiful sight, and I just can't let this one slide.

"Listen I don't want to be that guy... but I'm not going to sit here and nod my head while you guys praise mentally ill transvestites and dual citizens for destroying a perfectly good country. It's so fucking boring at this point. The arguments have all been made. The debates have all been had. It's obvious that you guys are on your side about these things, and people like me, we stick to our side. The only thing we both can do is pray for some kind of civil war catalyst so then we can fight it out legally. Well not legally, just under the cover of darkness or chaos or whatever it might be. You can talk about how cool nine-year-old drag kids are for now, but when the time comes, don't be surprised about getting your teeth put on a curb."

I'm cut off by a stool tipping over as one of these faggot's girlfriends storms off in rage. The boyfriend sits still, bewildered by either her actions or mine. I decide not to finish my train of thought and turn to the bartender for a glass of water. Nobody picks the conversation back up. Nobody orders another drink.

Should have listened to Dale Carnegie this time around.

THE SMELL AND WAYS OF POOR

Poor people all tend to smell the same. Cheap spray-on scents (take a shower and wear aluminum-free deodorant), shitty laundry detergent (you don't need it), cat piss diluted by repeated dryer sheet exposure (don't own a cat). The poor always smell like those strange flea market stress remedies – the ones in the little glass bottles. The poor always smell like public transportation and in turn public transportation begins to smell poor. The poor smell poor, and the second they get a little bit of extra cash, they buy expensive things that still look or smell poor.

And they can't shop for their lives, either. They will pay five dollars for a bag of ten microwave-ready chicken nuggets rather than the seven dollars for a fair selection of fresh chicken cutlets, or just get double that amount at a butcher for four dollars. It's not about the ease of cooking, or the inability to do so, they just genuinely believe this is the smartest option. That's the worst part.

Not only do these meals provide lesser, more expensive portions, but they are loaded with horrible preservatives and strange, experimental USDA chemicals. Seed oil ridden body killers, shelf stable astronaut concoctions, things that would look fitting in an actual witch's cauldron. Those Tyson chicken bites could last centuries or a voyage to Neptune and back, meaning they are probably not safe for human consumption. Granted we all tend to eat things like this once in a while, but this is where the poor divide themselves. They exist entirely on these foods. This is why the poor stay poor. This is why the poor stay fat and ugly. If you see someone poor or someone on this kind of diet, and they look attractive, you must save them however you can. Show them the way out and rescue their genetics before food alters them forever.

In the grand scheme of things, we are all victims. Soy, anti-nutrients, plaque, and viscous chemicals run ample in our blood. It manipulates the very code that makes us, us. We are being weakened, made docile for whoever yells the orders next. Nothing is truly safe to eat anymore unless you exile yourself to a forest and physically choose and kill what enters your stomach — or know someone who does that. When it comes to modern food, there is only really bad and sort of bad.

The grandmasters don't want us dead, they want us weak and subservient, obviously. This is nothing new, but finding out exactly what does it, well that is new. Fluoride in the water, hormones in the milk, gender dysmorphia in the air.

A CLOSER LOOK AT ASIANS

Asians — the world's leaders in revolutionary technology and whatever other garbage shit nobody needs around. For the past couple years, I've often found myself thrown off when thinking about these people who I can't quite figure out. Asians leave me with the same feeling I get after imaging being left to float alone in outer space, forever.

I see them in the same way I see a bored video game player. You have someone who's played Grand Theft Auto so much that he's exhausted all the normal ways routes of continuing. He's beat the whole game, but something keeps him there (maybe he feels there's nothing better), and so he finds a new approach. He breaks the boundaries and walls, glitches through the floors and ceilings, grants himself immunity and infinite resources, etc. The normal playstyle is now foreign to him, he's circled back around and sees everything as exploitable. Asians see real life this way, or at least this is what I believe.

I sat online for hours once, enamored by videos of this Asian guy making razor-sharp knives from a bunch of unexpected materials. A knife made out of cardboard, a knife made out of glass, a knife made out of ice, a knife made out of noodles — and all so sharp you wouldn't believe it. Initially, I was impressed. This didn't last long, however, because the more I thought about it and the closer I inspected the videos, the more I began to ask a very simple question: why?

Anyone can easily explain it away as a hobby of his, but me being an introspective genius brain, refused to accept this as the end. From what I could see, he lived in a tasteful (probably expensive) apartment loaded with fancy appliances, set before a decent view. Full fridge, nice clothing, clean cut and obviously well-off enough to spend hours making knives from strange objects. So why? Not the best example to support my theory, but I like it nonetheless.

The knife videos were quickly displaced by a headline that caught my eye: **"CHINA TO LAUNCH ARTIFICIAL MOON INTO SPACE TO LIGHT THE NIGHT SKY"**.

Sure, but why? What the fuck compels someone, compels a tribe of people to do this sort of thing? There is already a moon. Why even do this? What the fuck?

I strongly believe that the existence of Asians, specifically the Chinese, is an affront to God. Whether you believe in the existence of a master creator or not, the fact remains that Asians refuse to pull the brakes. They refuse to stop and reflect, worried only about pulling back the layers of every imaginable aspect of life and seeing how they can modify or monetize it. Like the bored Grand Theft Auto player finds ways to fall through the game's floor, the Asians find ways to timidly deconstruct the standard order of life. But again, I ask why? I think it's likely that the Chinese do not have souls.

At least with the Jews it's pretty widely known that the sometimes strange, often sinister things they do are for an overall tribal gain. They are bound together by their sort of code or central text, The Talmud. They do what they do for financial gain, higher status, more control, so on. This is easily understood by most. But with the Asians, not only is their endgame unknown, but they do much more bizarre and confusing things. It's easy to understand why Jews would falsify pieces of Christianity when faced with 'extinction or survival at any cost'. It's easy to see how guys like Woody Allen and Roman Polanski got away with molesting teenagers. It's not so easy to understand why the Chinese are trying to put another moon in the sky. And so, you maybe see why this leaves me with a feeling similar to being left alone, drifting through open space.

Granted that the Asians are as smart as we believe, they are likely further ahead than the world could ever know. If technology capable of making and launching a fake moon is public, what sort of chicanery is going on behind the curtains? What are the Chinese, the Japanese, the whatever other slanted eye peoples capable of, really? I would bet lots of money I don't have that they control a lot more than we know. I would bet that same money that every four years, a group of gooky mega-aristocrats pick a random name from a hat, and the next that person is The President of the United States. Or maybe they pick the one that will give them the most bang for their buck, the highest level of entertainment for those next four years. Maybe the walls of their boardroom are totally invisible to the human eye, maybe nobody inside it ever dies, maybe they have some secret no one will ever know. As an extremely racist friend of mine says, "with ██████, never blink."[A2]

LEAN INTO UNTIL$_x$

We could rebuild old Greece. Knock down the skyscrapers, burn modern art, wipe blank the entirety of digitization. We can level housing developments and turn shopping centers back into forests. We could leave behind a world of impurity and pain. Arguments settled in sword fights. Television replaced by live theater. Everything is marble and nothing hurt. We could tell the time via sundial and we could raise our precious young in the purity of sunlight. We could sleep and wake as our bodies felt. We could finally look up and see stars again. They would reflect in our eyes, guiding the way when memory couldn't. Then, just as this all becomes routine to us, we burn it all down and start again.

We were born too late. Too late to see the sun set behind massive pillars of stone and marble. Too late to see the greatest warriors of all time. Too late to feel the chilling uncertainty of how the world truly was, how the world truly came to be. Too late to set sail among oceans that promised either untold findings or a watery grave. Too late to live as intended.

We missed the time when a lonely traveler looked up at the moon and had absolutely no idea what it was. Sure, he could look through a telescope and better see the surface, but he'd never get rid of that overwhelming never knowing. It's like staring into the ocean at night. Calm like the dead or not, it's terrifying because you know it's so much larger than you can ever comprehend. It's worrying because you know a few dangerous creatures lurk just beneath. Even still, you stare into it and sway back and forth til it dizzies you. The ocean is one of the only man-shadowing frontiers we have left. It's an abyss, in every sense of the word. I find it more chilling than any gaze into space. Space isn't "here". The ocean surrounds us all, forever, immediately so. Space is a spook even to the people that travelled it. The ocean carries immeasurable levels of terror and wonder, especially at night. It holds secrets of the world past, treasures of the men before, and forfeits neither without a fight.

Atlantis and her people are still alive, uninterrupted by modernity. You won't find them because they don't want to be found. The ocean might always protect her.

We will never live in a period when there were no easily

accessible peer-review studies for every imaginable thought. There were very simple, very basic instances of life that could set straight every hair on the thinking man's head. And the further we go back in time, the harder it is for me to imagine just how beautiful things could be. I want to know what it's like to not understand a single thing about the universe surrounding; to look at stars in the sky and be absolutely floored by the possibilities. Are they bugs? Are they others like me, lighting fires for warmth? Are they smaller suns? Why does that large white circle turn ever so slightly along with them, all in unison? Are they moving or am I?

Imagine the Earth without a single piece of manmade garbage to disgrace it. We fucked this place up. We fucked it up and we made up stories to justify it and quiet the ever-searing guilt. There's a grand creator and his son died for our sins, so that makes it okay to cover ripe soil with weed farms, department stores, and porn studios?

We need to stop building, stop dysgenic breeding, stop removing ourselves from nature. This argument is old news, however. You're a hippie to desire a more environmentally-conscious population. You're an eco-terrorist to be so angry over the ruin of nature that you'd kill to end it. Protecting nature is embarrassing to most; a joke that anyone can laugh about in total avoidance.

It used to be okay to kill in the name of something reasonable. Someday that kind of thinking will come back. It always comes back. Has to come back.

"Hell is other people."

SCIENCE FICTION NOVEL

I haven't slept in five entire days and the world is a Ray Bradbury novel with way more obesity. Have you ever felt how great this feels? I feel it and I feel great. Not sleeping for this long grants you with unlimited strength at the same time as having zero strength. You are float.

It's a safe bet that I shouldn't be driving like this but I am and completely forgot where to. Music at its loudest makes my vision shake, and at its quietest makes me nervous, uneasy. I am totally aware of every breath exiting and entering my body and I am totally aware of everything happening around me. The best part is nobody knows that I've entered superhuman levels of sleep deprivation. I am awoked. I am alive. There's something in the water and it's killing us all but we deserve it. Rome fell. America too. Which is more embarrassing I don't know but I'll be long gone by the time we realize this all so I push onwards.

Fingers hovering the keyboard sound like candy unwrapping. Sudden loud noises sound are like gunshots, similar to how pain feels worse in the freezing cold. A man taps on his car door, waiting for the light to turn green and I hear snare drums bang. I took melatonin at three today to dig myself even deeper. And I don't touch receipts, I never touch receipts. They contain poison, gay poison, poison to make you gay poison. I try to read a book and the lines all pinch together. The words all look the same no matter how much space or difference between them. I have "read" the same sentence again and again, enough times to have just read the book itself. I bite celery and each closing down feels like a chore, but this amazes me so much that it's distracting, and no longer feels like a chore.

I avoid using cutlery because, in this state of absolute unrest, I know it would not end well. Five minutes after making this mental note, I shake myself from a slight dozing off to find I'm dicing up raw milk cheese. I don't know why — I only wanted to eat the cheese itself, so there was no reason to divide it up. There's really no reason for me to be awake for this long. I decided to do it out of curiosity and now I've become retarded, literally retarded. Is this what down syndrome is like? Every minute that passes I realize it feels like I'm keeping my balance upon a pirate ship. We're on some very rough waters. My shins are bruised from shifting pieces of cargo. Crates and barrels are smashing against the walls, and the contents blow away in the wind. Gunpowder? No, it looks more like a liquid, maybe brandy or something. Yes, liquid like me. There's nobody else on this ship. There's not even a captain or someone to steer us forward. This forty-foot gathering of wood and nails is at the mercy of the sea and its total indifference. Waves push us towards what I can only assume is land and then minutes later we are carried back out into the faceless fog. I drop a bowl on the ground and shattered glass shrapnel nicks my foot. I'm awake, still awake, lacerated. This warns me of that much. Or probably not, if that makes any sense. I make another mental note: The time is three-thirty PM and I've learned how to fall asleep standing up. The only reason I didn't is I forgot to starting how.-

There is a giant, and I truly mean giant island directly ahead of this hulking warship. Verily. Verily and with the wind. We crash on its shore and thank whatever unknown force made this so. There's no we, I soon understand. Just me.

Maybe it's six days, that I've been up.

All the precious ship cargo is destroyed by this point. Whatever was inside those crates and barrels belongs now to the stormy seas around me. Coconuts and appetizing berries cover the greenery behind a bed of white sand. I giggle and it carries on for so long that I start to fully laugh. My body shakes — not here, not on the island but in my kitchen of the real world. "Holy mother, why aren't you glad?" Or maybe they are both real worlds, which by now, I am confident about my ability to have achieved such a thing. I created a bridge between two dimensions in this sleep-deprived supermeltdown. How wild! I'd tell someone but I stopped talking about three days into this psychosomatic bender. I think more about it and decide I would never tell anyone. There's something telling me that telling them could take it all away. But the words just kind of say themselves rather than me choosing them carefully. I can smell smoke and it's definitely coming from deep within the woods. I've got a handful of berries that I eat while tip-toeing through the brush. My feet are bare but my feet are callused and strong. I've been doing this for a while in the pirate ship island world, I guess. I repeat myself a lot, in thought at least, because I don't talk. I stopped talking about three days into this adventure. The words just kind of –

The smoke was coming from a small campsite inhabited by exactly zero people. I'm not surprised as someone who single-handedly maintained the loneliest pirate ship for so many months. I wasn't necessarily mentally present for all that time, but the tally carved into our mast told me so. I'm the first to navigate around the tip of Africa, I tell me.

I'm making another bowl of diced raw milk cheese before I've even cleaned the broken pieces from my last effort. I can't tell the pieces of cheese and glass apart. I can't tell the floor tiles from the grout that divides them. I can't tell anyone about the vampire I found in the woods. Campfire not vampire. I can't figure out why I've been dicing the cheese up and putting it into bowls. That's two levels of resistance I needn't approach.

This means there is someone else here on the island, despite my ability to find them. I wonder what I'll say when I finally find them. My vocal cords are likely hoarse by now. I stopped talking about three days into this adventure. The words just kind of —

The campfire, pretty and calming. The campfire, I sit on a log nearby and lay my head on a pile of elephant ear leaves stacked high upon it. The smoke smells brilliant, sedates me until a jolting realization that I've diced too much cheese into the bowl back in cheese world. There's cheese and glass and blood all over the place and I really wish that someone else would just clean it up and not say a word to me in the process. Verily so.

I can hear the mailman outside but I don't think I'm expecting any packages. I wish him well as the mail truck starts off, and I pray that his cargo isn't thrown around wildly like mine. The mail truck is way smaller and obedient compared to my massive pirate ship. I'll give him some tips if he so requires them, but I think he's fine. The cheese is still spilling over the edge of the counter. The smoke is still filling up in my lungs while I nap. I feel nothing bad.

I wake up on the floor of my room and I am as confused as confused can possibly be. I don't remember falling asleep, let alone making it back upstairs. I don't remember what day it is, or even the month for that matter. Sleep deprivation is no easily-conquered drug.

IN THE SPIRIT THAT IS
CERTAIN OF ITSELF

Shoulder first, I barge through the back door of Serpico's, a pizza place a few blocks from the Allenhurst Beach. New Jersey is cold and disgusting. I have no idea why anyone with the option to leave wouldn't do so.

Three cops sitting at the table by the window, laughing and scarfing down plain slices, on the house of course. They have a big night ahead of them. Using four individual squad cars to detain a couple fifteen-year-olds who took the railroad shortcut home from the beach. Hesitantly releasing an old woman who's been pulled over for doing five miles-per-hour over the limit. Conducting delicate recon operations on the basketball courts. The life of a cop here in the infinitely crime-ridden, beachfront city of Allenhurst is nothing short of mortifying. I know. I know. It's so typical to hate the police, but I swear I have better reasons than the unwashed, dreadlocked masses.

I barge in through the back door and lean against the tile wall, a corner just before the restaurant opens up into the main dining area. I pull a Glock Nineteen (extended magazine, thirty-something nine-millimeter bullets) from underneath my belt and rack the slide. I wrap my arms around the corner, stiffened at full extension, and the rest of my body follows in perfect collusion. First shot is dead accurate, killing the cop who was most likely to notice me entering. Second shot is the same, another down. The third shot is rushed and strays wide. I've missed the third cop entirely and he's quickly fingering the level-three retention locks on his holster. He's carrying a Glock Seventeen, the slightly larger version of mine. He's also still yet to get it off his belt. I rush to stop him and bring the butt of my pistol down on his head. He's very stocky and it stuns him but not much else.

The next shot isn't one of mine. I'm bleeding from the hip because he too shot wide, only scraping my side. I press my stomach into the barrel of his gun, jamming it. This close together, neither his pistol nor mine can fire, so I wriggle my left arm free from the tangle. Grabbing my ankle gun with my left hand (Smith & Wesson snubby revolver in thirty-eight special) I unload the first three rounds into his stomach and the remaining two into his face as he falls backwards. He collapses into me as I let go of his collar.

The shop owner is standing perfectly still with his arms in the air. This is New Jersey and he's probably unarmed behind that shattered glass counter. Fucking gun laws, sorry man! His execution comes after a few minutes of my reassessment of the chaos around me. I exit out the same door I broke in through. No police respond to the scene because it didn't happen. I'm waking up from a nap in the sun, and my skin is hideously burned. That is the absolute truth. I'm absolutely sure I'll ■ in the future, outside of just daydreams. Absolutely and most definitely.

BORN INTO FIRE_x

It killed others, what makes you think it won't kill us? It won't just do that, it will ravage us. It will rape us senseless, to the point where everything we respect and care for is degraded in such horrible ways that we never see the same again. The future we are headed towards is one full of disgust beyond human comprehension. There are endless ways it can strike and that it will. But it's okay because we deserve it.

This is what we get for building robots to suck you off in a cocktail bar. This is what we get for turning our eight-year-old sons into women. This is what we get for turning everything into something you can fuck. This is what we get for sexualizing everything and saying okay. This is what we get for sleeping with so many people that it becomes hard to remember the last. This is what we get for too much meaningless play, not enough meaningful work. This is what we get for making everything readily available, to everyone, anywhere.

The only cleansing agent is fire; widespread and unending. Let it wash this planet out. Fight fire with fire until it's all pure again.

Realistically, there is nothing left to live for. In our effort to ease the burdens on humanity we've made the creation and raising of worthwhile human life an absolute gamble. Modern technology allows the weak to not just survive, but flourish. I say flourish in their sense of the word, not mine. Nihilism breathes down your neck as you realize that spending time with your beloved daughter didn't stop her from sleeping with her every coworker at that electronic music startup in Brooklyn. It didn't stop her from getting blackout drunk in a wine lounge and tearing her off clothes, fully & happily exposed to the entire establishment.

Most often, the worst of this new pain is within ourselves. We are born into this mess, and by that alone, we are impure. This is the kind of world baptism can't fix. This is the kind of slime that good upbringing can't wash off. This is the kind of pain medication can't stop. It all requires fire and only fire. It's in and on every single one of us. Born into sin, through sin, with sin, and only collecting more as the days linger on. Today's kind, they collect sin like bugs on the windshield of a barreling eighteen-wheeler.

I feel the urge to destroy, to hurt, to rape, to hunt, to abuse, to ambush, and be ambushed so I can react with violence. To all things, a desire to respond with violence. It's growing and growing and growing. Growing more when I reject more. Thanks to damaged women provided by the effortless dating market, I can act on that urge with absolute consent. But every time I do it gets worse. Every time I do it I realize how much more I am capable of, how much darker this all could get. Soon after it does, it gets much darker, and as expected there's someone ready to take it in with pleasure. This is where disgust t-bones ambition. The collision is bloody, no doubt a result of burnt out streetlights. The scraping metal cries harmonious. It sounds like Heaven weeping.

Just when you think it's all plateaued, the stakes are raised yet again. We humans are capable of impossible feats. Discovering fire, birthing kingdoms, landing on the moon, and yes, unlimited variations of sexuality depravity. It'll end when we do.

DAYTIME, DAY

Not sure which, probably Wednesday. Whenever you've lost yourself in the week it always tends to be Wednesday. Or Thursday. It could very well be Thursday.

Regardless of this minor detail, I am on the way to return a book to a woman. Her name is also a minor detail. I'm tired of committing non-essential females to memory, especially ugly ones. There is no 'friendship' between men and women, only the times where you think about having sex and the times when you are. You could argue that an ugly girl could be a man's friend. You would be half correct because, by law, she's potentially a man.

I get to her house and park my car. The driveway is just rocks and nothing has been done to make the area look more pleasant. Stepping inside I notice that there are two girls sitting on the couch, one on her phone, the other on her computer. I don't know why, but this is a strange sight to me. You don't see girls lounging around like this anymore. Girls are always on the move. It's part of what makes them seem so important. They are rushing, walking fast, eternally late to some appointment. They act like they don't have time for nonsense. Notice I said "seem" important. In reality, they are just extremely bad at time management and only have about one quick obligation per day that becomes so mangled and drawn out to the point of creating stress. Girls, alone and outside the home, are manic furnaces.

Making my introduction, I'm already handing the book over and heading out.

"You're leaving?" she cries out.

I nod inquisitively, implying that I don't see why I shouldn't be. I've been trying to speak less because it's mysterious and cool. It's not really, but I don't feel like talking today. I'm not at my usual level of confidence after earlier, in the car, I noticed that I'm a piece of shit.

"Let's go out tonight, yeah?" She begs in a tone that reminds me of how the British talk. For a moment in time, I feel like I just entered some Doctor Who episode. Who ends statements in that questionable tone? Why…? Yeah…? What a fucking idiot. If she wants to talk like Tom Baker, I'll compliment the role by hanging her from that long scarf he wears.

"I can't. I have to work late tonight."

I don't have work tonight, I don't even have a real job most days, but those words came out on their own as I realized she'd only ask if today was Friday. She's not the type of girl to drink on a weekday. I'm thrown off by this. Relieved too.

She says something back but I'm already closing the door behind me. It's Friday and I was nearly certain it was Wednesday. Is it the Friday that follows the Thursday I thought I was in last time I forgot the day? That could not have been yesterday because I'd remember this more easily. Then again, I haven't been sleeping well, so it could be yesterday. In that case, today being Friday would make sense. After all of this, I see the date on my phone screen. It's Thursday. I am tearing apart at the seams, honest to God, because this realization coupled with the fact that I've forgotten phones tell you the date. More than enough to ruin this beautiful afternoon.

"I must have read a thousand faces. I must have robbed them of their cause."

ASLEEP AT A STOPLIGHT, AWOKEN ONLY BY HORN

"Oh well, until then it's okay to have some faith in revolution."

Breathe in and wait for my signal. I can see them wrapping shaky hands around the rope guardrails. Their bridge is overdue for collapse. Every gust of wind pushes it effortlessly, almost like a flag or something equally light.

Breathe out and continue to wait. You can probably see them now too, can't you? They have war-torn rifles tied carefully to their chests and satchels full of tools. Their eyes have seen combat, real combat, for a lifetime. If they reach where they intend to go, they'll take the entire temple down by nightfall. If we reach where we intend to go, they'll die.

Breathe in and follow my footsteps, quietly. The creeping rise of adrenaline that comes with this sort of delayed, stutter-step chaos is so therapeutic to us both. I know you feel the same because our hearts beat together in time. Our chests rise and fall like kids trying to sleep through a thunderstorm. Our blood rushes back and forth like so.

Breathe in, breathe out, breathe in, hold. Keep holding, I think this is where we move. We may just have enough time to push forward. The adrenaline is flowing faster now and I'm skipping over whole words, entire thoughts even. I'm dancing around multiple ideas in my head. Follow me, as quietly as you did before, and make sure you are ready.

Our weapons are loaded. Hers and mine the same. We flank the ones we watched before from a path beside the bridge's exit. We are so close I can smell the dried game meats from inside their satchels. I can smell the rust on their knives. We breathe together and aim. We breathe together and pull the rifles back down to our chests. We breathe together and aim again. We

73

breathe together and pull back.

There are times I'm simply pretending I know a lot about these things. Times when I'm almost faking it till I make it. In this case, a government-contracted mission to execute government-contracted rebels gone astray, I like to think I know just enough. We breathe together and aim down the sights. This time, when we pull the rifles back to our chests, the barrels are hot. Four rebels, rebels that went against someone's orders, lay dead in the jungle. Gunshots and the soundtracks of war are all too common here. With this, we have no worry of being found out.

It's a long run back to the extraction point. We start towards it, only after she turns to me with a pleasant kind of sigh.

"Oh well... until then, it's okay to have some faith in revolution."

She said this already. Things are repeating, and getting much louder too. Horns are blaring. Multiple horns are blaring and getting much louder too. I jolt awake to a green light. I'm back on my way to wherever I was going. Tanning probably.

THE INTERNET BEFORE I DELETED IT

I'm back to normal, I'd say. I have a routine and a respectable sleep schedule. That or I'm so deep inside a sleep-deprived daydream that I've entered believable stages of a new dream world. Both are preferable to the third option: I could just be dead.

I'm signed online, scrolling down for anything interesting at this point.

One of my high school classmate's boyfriends died from

heroin. The post and the comments that follow are nothing but undeserved sorrow and praise. Was he a great kid? Not really. He kind of sold deadly narcotics to fifteen-year-olds, made rap music, and stood at a grand total of five-foot-five.

I comment, "Good riddance."

Instantly I'm being replied to with levels of disgust I haven't seen in weeks.

"What the fuck is wrong with you, asshole."
"Scumbag…"
"Come back to town and watch what happens."

These are the grammatically sound versions of what was said to me. I understood what I was getting into by commenting though, so it's okay.

I click on the newly deceased's profile and go through his endless amounts of pictures, memories, whatever. He looks like shit, probably smelled like shit, and died in the corner of high school party he probably wasn't invited to, shooting up dope he probably didn't pay for. I say give me rights to the funeral arrangements so we can bury this dead faggot in a ditch full of syringes and slut vomit like he deserves. In place of a flower-draped portrait, we can just have pictures of the heroin tracks that ran down his arms. Hopefully the mortician can brush those out.

His family will pay their respects to their degenerate faggot son who drugged up so hard that police found him in a puddle of his own shit and piss. Respects rightfully paid. I'd say throw his ugly corpse in the ocean, but that'd be marine pollution on par with the Exxon Valdez. Fuck you, you dead dope-dealing faggot scum. I hope everything Dante wrote about the depths of Hell is real, and more so, I hope you're making his experience look like a trip to the Brooklyn Zoo. Your girlfriend looks stupid when she cries over you, and if I see her when I'm back home, I'll cave her face in with the heel of my boot. I'll get away with it too, and whenever it is they post her Facebook commemoration, I'll be waiting there at the keyboard, ready to say something hilarious about her too.

CYCLE DEEPER, SLEEPY SLEEPER

Two days in on a standard sleeping schedule with a standard life routine. I never really explained how it goes down because I went off-track.

Five AM – Wake up refreshed, usually. Raw liver.
Five-fifteen AM – Raw milk and maple syrup, warm up to lift.
Six AM – I'm generally done working out around this point.
Seven AM – But it can go a bit longer. I don't stop until the sweat builds so heavily in my eyebrows that it pours into my eyes. Burning eyes means time to shower soon after.
Seven-thirty-five AM – Shower. Or did I do this already? Gurgling.
Three-thirty AM – I'm realizing I've said all of this before and I'm starting to question my stability. I've said this before, right? I'm not wrong to believe this.
Three-thirty-three AM – I'm awake at three-thirty in the morning, writhing on the floor in pain. I thought this pile of little white thumbtacks was ibuprofen and I swallowed a handful. The deeper they bury themselves in my digestion tract, the sharper the pain becomes. Funny enough, now I could really use some pain pills. I dry heave and blood stains the carpet that's sometimes beneath me, sometimes above me. "Not exactly dry," I say quietly to myself, after a moment of trance. Something pulses in my abdomen. Not thumbtacks, but a sort of gut feeling. Ha ha ha. It tells me to act.

I coil my fingers together into an arrowhead shape and jut them through my skin, piercing into my stomach. Inside, I pass yet another layer into what I can only imagine is the intestines. I feel four small thumbtacks. They laugh at me with mischievous, smirking faces as I pull them out and toss them into the trash. My wounds self-repair within the same moment. I breathe and search a different cabinet for pain pills. I find them and send them down the hatch.

I'm doubled over in pain again. I think I swallowed more tacks. No, no. These are small rocks. Small white pebbles rattling against the walls of my already aching guts. I sit down and bring my knees to my forehead, rocking back and forth in tempo with the waves of discomfort.

A trojan horse waits just outside my door, and I am well aware of who's inside.

"We come in peace, sire."
"No you don't, and if you keep lying, you'll swallow these too."

Whoever's leading the horse pounds again.

"Did you hear what I just said?" I shout.
"No, say it again."
"Go away."

At the exact second he starts pounding again, a dismal synth keyboard warbles behind me. What a miserable, tone-deaf song. It's something you'd hear during the latest hours of The Weather Channel. Even worse than that.

"What's that?" The trojan horse man persists.
"You heard me, I said go away."
"What's that music?"

I ignore him, as I've reached my limit for small trojan horse man chicanery. I think I forgot to mention he's tiny and so is his army. About half the height of a standard household door.

After minutes of the song continuing, someone finally starts speaking. It's a sing-songy voice, not quite singing though.

"No point. No worry. Nothing to keep pushing on towards."

I'm confused, even more so when another voice joins in.

"Not I, nor they, could muster up the words. Lay down and take it. Breathe it all in. Soon the moon comes along for a swim. A dip in the pond of stars — and then it's gone. Like dresses on sale in summer, you're a hatred baby."

Another pause.

"More medicine, to cause the cause that cures the cure. Happenstance is hands."

I take the desk chair beside me and send it barreling through where I assume the sound plays. It doesn't stop. I pick up the desk chair again and smash open the window, climbing down the side of the house using only its panels and my heavily-trained grip strength.

TUESDAY, ACTUALLY THIS TIME

I'll be the first to admit that these daydreams are getting out of hand. I'll also be the first to admit that I'm not sure if I've been sleeping or working out or awake. At this point, I've fallen into what I like to call "a very real but tolerable Hell". This is the kind of existence where reality feels light in weight, not a single thing to ground you. Everything glimmers as if it laid upon the beach midday. Everything is quiet until it's too loud. All electricity hums, echoes, and crashes back into itself. It is invisible alive. Electricity is a ghost.

It is bad, this much is obvious. I am physically and mentally lost in the spell. I encourage you to at some point try sleep deprivation as a drug. You will cross paths with yourself. You will see waves of deathwater. Removal of sleep means the sun sets on time, in front of you.

WEDNESDAY, AND
PLEASE LET IT BE REAL

I've been dragged to an Applebee's through some impressive level of extortion or otherwise. Sitting in a booth, I take in that crisp Applebee's air and understand what it's like to be a piece of shit.

Across from my table is a family that can't seem to stop smiling. I should be appreciative of this, a wholesome family, braving the piss-storm with teeth out throughout, but I'm not. The reason I'm not is because of the father and his stupid decision to wear what he perceives as "nice dinner attire" to a fucking Applebee's. A brown houndstooth sports coat over an Izod polo tucked into stonewashed Levi's boot cut jeans, held up by a Docker's belt and topped off with white New Balance's. This is his Sunday best, on Wednesday. The wife and children are wearing generally normal clothes.

Why am I annoyed? I'm not. I wouldn't say annoyed, more so intrigued while still death gripping a dull butter knife.

He's clearly dressed up for this, I know full well it's not his usual attire. He dressed up to pay absurd prices for food that is nearly advertised as "Yes, we fucking microwave it, what are you going to say? Don't microwave it? We already did." It's not only this but the fact that only two minutes down this very road is a family-owned restaurant with much cheaper food. Food that is cooked using real ovens and real stoves. But no, Jerry Russo from the local Honda dealership took his family to this disgusting, chemical-ridden death trap. Applebee's translates to Auschwitz. This sick fuck has growing children to feed and he's shoving microwaved chicken bites into their smiling mouths. They trusted him. Their mother trusted him. I trusted him. The waitress, if you could even call her that much, nears the table to take his order.

"I'd like the Ribeye steak, well done," he says with confidence so thick I can only grab the butter knife tighter, I can only wonder where he gets it from. I am sick.

I can't hear the waitress reply, too soft-spoken, but I imagine she asks him how he'd like his steak microwaved. Microwave the sides too, please. Microwave the check before you bring it out. I'll make sure to leave a big tip if you promise to microwave it and charge fourteen ninety-nine for the burned remains. Double that, add an appetizer and we've got a commercial-worthy deal on our hands. Their hands, I mean. I don't want Applebee's blood on my hands. The industrial revolution was a fucking disaster; Applebee's is proof of this alone. Microwaved martinis are two for five all night but you are only allowed to have three. The foods they serve cold? Microwaved and then left to chill in unclean industrial freezer. Applebee's microwave holocaust, come in now before it's too late. Six million dead chickens, six million well-done steaks, no nutrient content to be found, help us it's the end. Then we have Chili's…

ACCELERATE THE WORLD, DECELERATE YOUR TRIBE.

Inhaling two large Red Bulls has put me into total maniac deathmode. I'd kick a hole through my own neck if I had insurance to cover it. I don't have insurance. I don't even know how or where you go to get it, without being dragged into debt of course. Maybe that's student loans I'm thinking of.

Credit scores are an assclown's game, a faggot's number. Something only a desk jockey jerk-off would concern himself with. You either have enough money to buy something or you don't. Your credit score is hollow, on par with last night's sports scores, what the stock market closed at, and how many stars your local quiche bar has. Your credit score is unimportant, similar to the number of dates you are supposed to go on before dropping the n-word.

Normal people laugh and think about the idea of accumulating massive debt before committing suicide. Normal people laugh and never do it. They should though. Do this right away if you feel life is going nowhere, but do it when you're older if you feel like sticking around longer. Paying bills? That's for saps.

If you won't get arrested for not paying it, don't pay it.

End of chapter — forgot the rest. Hold on, no. I know.

Just sucked down a room temperature cold brew and kicked two holes through the front desk of Berg & Berg Law Firm. The receptionist is so frantic that she actually thinks she's calling the police. She's not because the phone cord was cut clean by jagged wood shards. Yet another example of my ability to observe all things mission-critical, even in the midst of chaos. I'm on fire tonight, at some points literally. I have become acceleration. Want more detail? Acceleration isn't just causing problems and watching the world contort in reaction. Acceleration is about causing problems the right way, the smart way, the kind of way that keeps you out of jail, because you can't move forward when you're chained down. Nietzsche said that evolution doesn't necessarily mean progress, that just because we changed it doesn't mean we changed for the better. Well when I say "to accelerate" or "to push forward" or "to lean into", I don't mean towards a better world – not immediately at least. We are leaning into the collapse. We are pushing for the ignition of cleansing fire. I am acceleration and I am the reaction. This way nobody knows who's doing what or why. I am the one dumping magazine after magazine into a crowded gay nightclub and I am the fat black woman with DMV-phenotype who thought it'd be naughty to party with her gay friends that night.

I am the world's fire and I am the world burning. This is acceleration and reaction forever until it can't happen anymore. Or until it doesn't need to happen anymore. That's how it goes and you don't get to say otherwise if you disagree. The Butterfly Effect is a vicious and deadly thing. It could get me just the same as you or anyone else.

Don't drink energy drinks. Don't drink any of them. Not even coffee. The more you drink, the more you disrupt your gut microbiome or your natural energy supply or your soul, to put it boldly. All of a sudden, from out of left field, you feel like committing some serious suicide. Get your energy from a good diet. Be a man, rely on no substance. Abuse yourself in other ways.

WHEN YOU SLEEP, MY BLOODY VALENTINE

Soaked in reverb, obscured by strange noise and poor vocal quality.

"When I look at you, oh, I don't know what's for real…"

Not much compares to this single song. It has a certain magic.

PULL BACK THE CURTAINS

They say to always hide your true knowledge so that the world never figures what you really know, what you really believe it, and then use it against you. I say always hide your true knowledge because you're not as smart as you think and sometimes you may confidently pronounce Goethe as "Goethh" during a star-studded dinner.

RENEGADE ANTI-ALCOHOLISM.

I don't drink alcohol. I find that among other reasons, it is one of life's ultimate cop-outs. Recall the part in Dante's *Inferno* when he noted that towards the end of Hell, some men went down before they had even died. How their earthly bodies were hollowed out and replaced with a demon until said body's true "death". How their soul itself was relegated to the frozen lower ditches, unable to move for eternity. This is how I see alcohol, recreational or otherwise. Not to mention that beer is estrogenic, extremely high on the glycemic index, and contains gluten. That, paired with the way it's consumed throughout the entire course of the night, intermittently, is a nightmare for your blood sugar levels. To drink casually is to accept an early and ugly death. To do that while also being an embarrassing drunk is something else.

Drinking, if it has to be done, should be celebratory. Not for a promotion at your chain restaurant. Not because it's the end of the work week. Not because you're bored. Grow up.

TWO THOUSAND SEVEN, THE END

Or relatively close to it. There are mountains of evidence to support this claim. RuneScape never gets any better. Emo kids become harder to find. Computers get too complicated, phones too complex. YouTube realizes its true potential and, for purely selfish reasons, pasteurizes what could have killed television entirely.

The Nineties were the final stand, a final frontier of culture worth embracing. Kind of. It was brimming with innocence and tastefully reinvented Americana. Kind of. No other time has ever replicated its method of attraction. Kind of. There's a reason that so many people my age attach themselves to the time period. It's simple – the nineties did not end until Hurricane Katrina washed it all away. Not even nine-eleven pulled off a feat that large. Still prefer it never happened, though.

LUNAR FRIDAY

It's Friday night. The weather is perfect. The wind interlocks with itself like some new jute twine and the sky resembles a crystalline thief. Having spent enough time around people this week, I justify now sitting in. I am my friend, an inside friend, one who craves something like a dark lunch. Sleep strikes.

I'm outside. Bach pours from the house's twin oak doors. I'm pacing around a lily-spotted garden, pointing a shotgun at the police standing behind my fence, singing along. I'm pacing around the cooling moonlight and humming along.

"Put your gun down," they plead.
But why would I? It's *my* gun.

"They call me the believer, and I'm never coming back!."

BEFORE THE FUTURE GETS TOO LOW$_x$

Do you want to know what the future looks like? Of course you do. Underweight college hermits masturbating to bored-porn because it's closest to personal experience. Soy and nut milk delivered intravenously in school libraries that resemble FEMA camps. BPA-bong death overdrive. Sexual depravity passing heart disease as the leading cause of death. Tesla Motor death camps. Public dubstep handjobs. Homeless concerts. Elon Musk selling 3D self-suck virtual reality zip downloads, sponsored by Sony, the newest Zuckerberg acquisition. Frozen insect dinner ads. Robots laughing you out of your coal mining job. Your fingernails taste more like food than food tastes like it used to. They really want you to start eating bugs. Suicide passing sexual depravity as the leading cause of death. Government cutting into your music with nuclear warnings. Warnings become the most played song. Songs don't sound very different anymore. They want you to love eating bugs.

Uber drivers double as deep state spies, reporting the locations of even the most lightly suspected cyber criminals. Israeli sleeper cells awaken to kill other Israeli sleeper cells. Saudi princes holding the majority share of America. Cointelpro run by ex-slave hoejabi immigrants. NASA enforcing the death penalty. Breath tax, violence tax, piss tax. Video game streamers reading CIA headlines. Mixed race cereals and protein bars. Homeless senators and congresspeople.

Breathing hurts, we know this much, but we can't remember the last time it didn't. Names are usernames. The color spectrum is black. Former freedom walks eyes down the gallows. There's more conflict in the Middle East. Conflict in the Middle East drags out so long and so powerfully that it expands into Europe, which is kind of already the Middle East at this point anyways, so nobody notices. Trying to make war in the Middle East seem cool.

The streets of Paris, once romanticized by literary titans, now covered in a carpet of brown immigrants; the Seine overflows with native tears and the semen of rape. Rockefeller merges with Rockefeller. Many report, few listen. The Washington Post is the Washington Examiner. CNN is FOX. The National Review is still a gang of limp-wristed faggots with dual-citizenships and hispanic preteen fetishes. Conservatives giddy to confiscate guns and style. Another war in Iraq. Oh you don't want to serve your country? The "I" in IED stands for Israel.

The future isn't world peace. The future is a spiteful coworker deepfaking videos of you masturbating on the clock. It's the microchip in your arm "accidentally overheating" because you catcalled the airport trash robot. It's your parents being buried in the cloud courtesy of Google. It's your children asking why restaurant menus aren't on a touch screen. It's your grandparents asking why your children are so retarded. It's your grandchildren being diagnosed as gay in the womb. It's your vape not working because you put too many apps on it. The future of now is Jeff Bezos giving you two-day free shipping on a pile of wet dicks with which to go fuck yourself, forever and eternally. The future is gay cops on fire.

There was a time when some of us cared about the tailspin. Here, now, not a single person cares about it. It happens again tomorrow. "That's the name on our washing machine, right Mommy?" "Yes, and our car too. And the computer. And the weather machine." It hurts to care. Our eyes face forward or the boots come down. The police are not our friends but then again they never were. Now they are military-grade bullies, before they were only arrogant high school washups. Consensus says the people prefer the bullying kind of police, simply because it's nice to feel some form of "compassion", regardless of its harsh approach. They prefer the tough love instead of none at all. The consensus is never released to the people. We didn't reach this nightmare by telling the truth.

The future sounds bad, doesn't it? Interestingly enough, this future isn't so future. It's more "tomorrow" than "too far to see". We often understand the course we are set upon, but do nothing to stop or improve it. Any normal person sees terrible darkness ahead and assumes: "The general population must be perfectly okay with what's going to happen. Why else would they be so calm?" And this normal person's rationale may end here as they join the crowd. But in the event it doesn't end there, their attempts at salvation will likely fall upon on deaf ears. Deaf ears with really loud mouths. Loud mouths that never stop yelling incorrect rap lyrics at their shitty friends in a shitty nightclub.

I'm not scared to reach this gash in the timeline anymore. The fringes of culture tend not to sway in the passing wind. It's actually more of a tornado full of lewd snapchat videos and the odor of ashen morals, like high school locker room sweat. Everyone will forget to cry over the things they've done wrong because they cried so much when they were first caught doing it. The air is pungent with tech conference body stink, open wounds, and Ciroc. It can't go on forever though, there's always something to realign the path of man. Maybe this time around it'll be me who becomes the wheel of fire. Maybe it's me who cuts the brakes.

The chances to turn back lessen in time.
Fear is the future unless it all burns now.

"Holy Mother
Why are you weeping?
Holy Mother
Why are you sad?"

THREE FEET ON THE GAS

I hear some people are buying extension ladders, going up on various store roofs, and pulling the disconnects on their heating and cooling devices. I hear that all the food inside goes rotten, costs the company many thousands of dollars. I hear that it causes problems whether or not the store carries food products.

I hear some people are buying tennis rackets and hitting medium-sized pebbles into wealthy and ethnic neighborhoods, from extremely far distances away. I hear some of the pebbles are smashing Escalade sunroofs, McMansion mega bay windows, and more. I hear nobody can figure out where it's coming from. I hear some people call the cops but nothing ever happens.

I hear some people are claiming to be repairmen, going inside offices, and leaving dead fish in the ceiling tiles. I hear some people are buying machetes in bulk and leaving them next to the homeless while they sleep. I hear some people are learning how to build handheld EMPs on the internet and shutting off people's electronics in secret. I hear people are buying burner phones and calling ambulances to places, over and over. I hear some people are throwing screws in news station parking lots. I hear some people are getting jobs and immediately quitting. I hear some people are feeding journalists completely false stories and making them look bad.

I hear some people are putting caution tape across busy streets and highways. I hear some people are filling public bathrooms with balloons. I hear some people are throwing eggs at synagogues. I hear some people are screaming in public. I hear some people are downloading dating apps, telling matches to meet them somewhere, and never showing up. I hear some people will do exactly that but jump them in a dark alleyway.

I hear some people are using high-powered lasers to burn things from far away. I hear some people are finding ways to buy dangerous exotic animals, then letting them loose in cities. I hear some people don't have enough to buy them and are forced to break into zoos and open the cages. I hear some people are sneaking booze into the coffee at Alcoholics Anonymous meetings. I hear some people are thinking about making a ██ ██ that caves New York City in on itself. I hear store and restaurant employees are quietly handing out door keys to anyone who asks.

I hear some people are running through car dealerships and smashing the windshield out of every one on the lot at night. I hear some people are hiding bluetooth speakers in places and broadcasting racial slurs at full volume.

I hear some people are making homemade explosives and knocking down cell towers. I hear some people are making homemade explosives and disintegrating local power substations. I hear some people are stealing construction machines and driving them into lakes.

ROMANTICISM GATEKEEPER

"Do you know how many Korean pop star pictures I had to go through to find one dimly-lit selfie? Too many. Now, if I had reached this selfie and been amazed with what I saw, then my efforts would prove necessary."

"I take it you didn't approve?"

"I wouldn't have sex with her, no. She was pale, not in the attractive way. Timid, not in the charming way. And poorly dressed, not in the ironic way. Some girls dress like shit and it kinda works, like Mac Demarco's girlfriend. But not this girl. She looks like the type of girl who's only waiting for marriage because she has 'social anxiety' and not because it's the correct thing to do."

"Some people are into that, you know."

"That's great, but I'm not one of them. I'm mostly bored of women. I'm aware of my capabilities with them and the more I have the more I want. Not even in quantity, but in both quality and depravity mostly. I think by the end of my twenties I'll be deciding which to date based on their appreciation of a knife to the throat. I'm thinking maybe we should all just start killing them. I used to feel excited and curious about each of the different girls before me in the world. Which one will I date for the week? This one has a nice apartment, this one buys me things, this one is the best looking this year. Now I'm looking at them all like food on a shelf, trying to remember if I've tried something similar to this one, or if I've ever ventured out enough to try that one."

"It seems to me like you need some alone time. Leave these tired monologues in your head, please."

"I've tried that, I promise you. I shouldn't be at this point. I haven't even done as much as other people my age, but I don't have to because they do more with less conviction. Behind everything I've said, every sin I've committed, every woman I've wronged, was absolute sincerity. The others don't do this and they suffer for it."

"I think you're getting a bit dramatic."

"Oh! Oh! Everything is dramatic when it's not interlaced with pretext these days. I could resolve every conflict in the world with a loud enough megaphone and the promise that nobody would call me a faggot and laugh. There's no substance behind words anymore. Mostly because we are all scared. Everyone is a widdle wolf wiff wounded paw, limping around with big teary eyes, but also pretending they aren't this and shut the fuck up dude."

"Mhm, right."

"I am suffering. You are too and you won't admit it."

BEWARE WHEN TODAY IS SATURN DAY

Like most every other day, I'm in flux between work and things that I think could benefit me in some way. We have moments where our consciousness slips into something dangerous and obscure. We hop from a train of thought and land in the weeds. It's in those weeds that we realize that it's hard to stand up straight. We realize it's hard to stand up straight because the train following closely behind the last has a lot stranger cargo and you're tempted to jump on. On the train I feel the confusion pooling in my ear canals, swishing around. The world is so strange and it'll never be fully understood, which is okay because smarter people before me have tried and fallen flat. Nothing matters until it does and then it doesn't.

The human timeline has stretched on far too long. We've overstayed our welcome here on Earth. Checkout was at noon and we're still in the room getting drunk and pillow fighting over things based in actual nothingness.

The longer this all goes on, the more room there is for ideas of the past to be misconstrued by the future. The longer time stretches on, the higher the waste pile stacks. It all rolls downhill, faster and faster, until some congresswoman is on television saying Plato would have been pro-Israel. There is only down from here for the people collective. Individually though, I believe we have some headroom to veer upwards. There's still time to cut away. There's a way to burn it all down and stay comfortable while doing so.

You can never fully defeat a human spirit if it wants to keep going. If something truly wants then it will want forever. I feel this way and I know many others do too. The day I'm torn into a million pieces and buried spurs only new plans of attack. What's left me will chase you down forever, and that scares people.

A LOWERWORLD AND ITS DEMONS

Why doesn't anyone realize we are living through the most abstract and depressing stage of human history? There is no period in the annals of time that we can point to and say "yeah, this has enough in common to be used as reference". We are alone in this Hell we built. We are adrift now in space, the final cord binding us to the ship now snaps under the pressure. "Apollo, do you copy." This sorry transmission will never make it, granted our higher power has any decency. We don't deserve to be heard at all, let alone our obnoxious death rattle.

From here we can only push outward into the absurdity, and there's no shame in that. Quitting is for losers and it'd be a sin to stop deteriorating now. Godless or not we'll perish. Whether or not sins exist, their punishments do. A world seeking a million ways to reject divinity's lure – and for what?

I'm tired though, tired of looking at it all. Tired of looking in this way I do. I'm here telling myself and anyone who will listen that the level of disreality we have reached is now unpredictable. Doesn't this mean that a spontaneous reversal of all things bad could happen a minute from now, or tomorrow, or next spring? This chaos isn't the worst thing to come down on us, simply because it has the potential to sway either direction. Maybe so.

I hope for this, I pray for this. I wish that tomorrow the world shines brighter but remains a cool and easy temperature.

I wish that tomorrow every song sounds better. I wish that tomorrow sugar stopped rotting our teeth. I wish that tomorrow the Earth spun a little bit slower, that the days and seasons lasted a little bit longer. I wish that tomorrow God checked in on his precious makings. Shook every hand, smiled into the glowing eyes of the heavenbound. Tomorrow, water feels like peace when it travels through your body. Tomorrow doesn't know about war and it won't for thousands of years. Tomorrow doesn't worry about its ancestors millennia ahead. Tomorrow doesn't worry about their future penchant for fire and death. Tomorrow like this doesn't come though, I very quickly realize, as I'm woken up by sirens. My neighbor died this morning. Everyone stares blankly at him being loaded into an ambulance, and as it pulls away, their bodies melt into their feet and slide into the lake beside them. Me, expert of the distinction between the dreamworld and real, understands that this is very much the product of a deep REM cycle. This tells me two things: (1) the dream could have personal significance, a hidden meaning, but I don't care because (2) I haven't fully woken up yet and the possibility of a brighter world could be waiting outside.

Either way, we still drift further from the ship. I guess it comes down to how much oxygen we have left, and how much we devote to hyperventilating versus how well we maintain composure, even just to see more of the beauty surrounding.

THE STARS DRAW ME CLOSER

I'd like to think I lean more towards the 'oxygen management' type. I say that I'd like to think this because in reality, it's not true. I'm too negative and I hate myself for it.

But today, wherever it is that I'm speaking from right now, I continue to drift out into space. There were others with me, but I'm afraid they have died along the way. I'm okay with this and I say that with chaste intent. My fellow astronauts were well-trained and understanding of the dangers involved. They were taught tirelessly, day after day, in the art of keeping calm even when faced with the harsh reality that is a slow death in space. They died with stars in their eyes, quite literally. They died with honor in their hearts. Somewhere along the way, some unidentifiable space calamity will swallow their bodies whole. Or maybe it will shred them apart. It could even transport them to another dimension. This much I do not know, but it excites me all the same. I don't know why I'm alive but I refuse to question it any further.

The time passes and it's hard to tell just how much exactly. I'm wearing a watch but it's under my space suit. I probably look so silly floating around out here. The aliens might be looking over and giggling into their bony green hands. They definitely don't speak English, so whatever little alien jokes they trade back and forth might have made me laugh too. The only thing that looms over me is the draining supply of oxygen. According to the calculations inside my ultra-smart NASA brain, it should have depleted a long time ago.

By way of divine intervention, I have transcended the need for oxygen in space. I pop the latches and seals on my big space helmet and throw it into the air, or whatever you call what's all around me. What is all around me? You never really understand the world 'universe' until you see what I'm seeing now. Imagine the feeling of walking through the ocean, coming to a sand bank's end, and jumping forward into the deeper unknown. There's no longer anything under you and it's impossible to tell just how far down that void goes. Well here, it never ends. At least that's what most research shows. I know this registers as strange to you because it does to me as well, a learned scholar of the astronautical arts. I kick my feet and hum a tune. There's no sound out here I remember. Still though, I'm producing sound waves aren't I? Where are they going? I'm willing to bet those tiny little green men picked them up. They're giggling at me again. This time it's because of my tone deaf tune. I let them have their fun, not much else I can do anyways.

There's a smile on my face as wide as this place is vast. The term "at peace" cannot describe what I feel. The days, or what I assume to be days, pass just as I wished they would. The air is cool on my skin and the farther I float outwards, the more absurd are things I see. Not too long ago I saw a planet that very closely resembled my home, Earth. If I could make touchdown there, I'd tell all the inhabitants of its land about the inhabitants of mine. I'd tell them about the wonderful music we make and the ways we get along. I'd tell them about the warmth of the sun and how it makes us dark when we love it too fondly. I'd tell them about the relations between our many tribes and doctrines of love. They tell me similar things, similar as similarities can be between two separate worlds.

"Have you no war, child of Earth?"
"War?" I ask earnestly.
"Yes, war."
"I'm afraid I'm not familiar with the term!" I cry out, excited to learn its meaning.

The inhabitants around me bow their heads for a moment. When they come back up, it's all smiles. In turns, they pat me on the back and flash me partly kind, mostly belittling expressions. The kind of expression a father gives his son when he asks where babies come from. But the child is too young to learn just yet, and this is how the tribesman here handle me.

"You not knowing is for the better," the leader of the tribe says to me. They all stand up, and taking the hint, I do too.

A few of them break from the pack and lead me down that same corridor of stone and wood I came in through. The place is beautifully constructed, by hand most likely. These aliens, aliens just a degree away from being Earth humans, have meshed their primitive architecture with modern era intelligence. The only earthly equivalence I can share is to have seen Leonardo da Vinci painting pictures of elk on the walls of a cave, but describing it to onlookers with all his known eloquence. Describing cave art in son langage de la renaissance, sa manière particulière. Should shock me, but doesn't. I have seen the wonders of space and the voids between them. I have lived where others could not; should not, really.

Now, it occurs to me. This could be the rest of my life! Exploring new and old planets, learning about the beasts upon them, what they've done in those times before me. I am the alien now. To them I am the stranger, and I like it this way.

Space isn't real though.

BE AU TIF E AL

Did you know? A void between us? Infinite space between personalities? Won't explain why because you know it to be true. But even here in this gap, we find always-changing pieces and parts, gears that steadily shift and allow for newly bourgeoning traits and likenesses to fit in. A few weeks ago, your stubborn girlfriend was painfully critical of some Japanese shoegaze band you stumbled across. Today, she sits before you, smiling after her fourth listen, just as you did on your first.

There's a sea of differences between us all, even the ones we think we're closest too. Voids between us where certain questions sleep. Would you rather kill or be killed? Where do you see yourself in five years? Are you ready to raise a family? Have there been cases where you dreamt about a girl who you haven't kissed then made it a point to kiss her in real life? For no reason other than to erect a bridge between this world and the dream one? A pizza party or pasta sleepover? This sea is rough. Its waves are plentiful and choppy, but that's just okay.

It's okay that we are different because once you finally interlock perfectly with someone who understands things the same way you do, you're capable of many things.

We are constantly aware of the divide. There's not a single moment that it doesn't bury itself into how we view a person, even more so in women. We watch and wait, preying upon body language and subtle remarks. Truth in jest, awkward laughter, a couple attempts to move closer. We watch and wait and watch. The number of thoughts that take flight when a woman compliments you on something you had just noticed about yourself. The way her perfume smells, half-hoping it's the kind that emanates through sweat born of nervousness, because once you start dating for too long, it'll likely retreat. It was fun while it lasted. It was more like a novel than fun actually, because we put a lot into it for the time we had. A firm and full booklet, dense with moments to hold. The new divide makes it horribly apparent that everything is over. She was thinking this when you were thinking that. She was thinking Thai food when you were thinking about blood sacrifices. She was thinking about a future together when you were thinking about her ass and thighs in a sundress. Always just a fraction of a hair away, not much in the larger picture, but still not perfectly aligned.

Maybe you don't want to perfectly align. Maybe you don't want to be intertwined soulmates. Maybe you are a Disraeli of the soul. Maybe you wish to come home and fall into the lap of some semi-maternal figure. Maybe you want nothing, forever.

To articulate love is to have misunderstood it. You are three streets down. But in the middle of finding love and not, there is a lot of pretending you did. With this comes the many realizations that she was only a special stranger the entire time. These sorts of things come only, as far as I've seen, in harsh absolutes. Absolutes that take root in the center of even larger absolutes. We are under the impression that we love sometimes because it is an emotional disorientation, and the second we halt that spinning motion, the mysticism is mostly gone. Well, usually. I believe that some people "master" the motions. They can replicate the dizzy feeling on command, or even delude themselves into its hold forever. Nothing describes this mess of potential and failed romances better than the word "melancholy". There's probably a better choice. In English, it seems we don't have very many words that combine two or three individual words. Especially not three feelings. Has a word ever covered four feelings? Four outcomes or four beliefs?

A week ago, I spent every single night with a woman who convinced me that she was perfect. She didn't say she was perfect, and she didn't make an overstated effort to do so. It just came across this way, and I was in agreement. The excitement of a having to prove your worth to a woman, who knows barely anything about you, adds much to the spinning. The dizzy twirl about. You use your little tricks and charms on her, and sometimes they work. She does the same to you and they work tenfold. You tuck her hair behind her ears and she lowers her head with a smile. It always happens like this. You kiss for the first time and you learn the rhythm she makes with her lips, then adapt to it. It always happens like this. You grab her by the hips and squeeze so hard that your fingertips can almost touch. It always happens like this, unless you've fallen in love with a fat girl.

This can last as long as a week or two, even longer if you're both sickly attached. There's lots of danger in that. It's called the halo period and nobody can take shelter from its glow.

The week or so long that it lasts will feel like countless beautiful moments heaved together by sweaty and nervous hands. Even the conversations between these moments were you praying that it goes as well as last time, solidifying that you'll see her again tonight, feel quickly passed by. These days seem pure and sometimes they aren't. I'd say they are more pure than most other human moments.

When it ends you'll barely even notice. There's rarely ever a sobbing fit or questioning the structure of yourself and the life you've made. At least not for the men in the equation. It doesn't always fade away, sometimes it's a dead stop. A message missed, forever. That's all it takes. One last thought exchanged between you two. In both cases though, you too easily accept the fact that she wasn't a girl you loved so deeply and cared so madly for. So madly that, at one point, you would have married and lived together forever. Despite the tired and late night discussions about having children and growing old in love, it never really happens. At least not with one another. The terrifying part isn't the sudden end but how quickly you signed your life away to a woman you had only just met. It is scary and it is beautiful.

Nothing bad comes of this – only more knowledge towards finding the one you never stop talking to. This is not the case for women, though. They become whores after too much of this process, or any of it at all. Beware of the woman who's seen too frequently the spoils of war. Romantic war. All romance is war. Love relies on tragedy, always.

Do you think I'm pretentious? I'm worried you might think I try too hard. I want to win your approval. Do you think I think I know everything about love? That would mean you think you know everything about love. And that you can safely say I don't. Have you mastered the dizziness? Or have you misunderstood its ways? You can't understand it because nobody ever really has.

THIS MONTH MUST END

Car accident. Not my fault. Someone in this building has that vape cough. I can hear it so clearly. Walking around. Refused any medical attention beyond minor surgery, called some doctor a pill salesman and he said I have to leave as soon as possible.

NATION'S CAPITAL

The thing about D.C. is that looking from the outside looking in, you'd think it's probably a real wild and interesting place. You'd think it'd be impossible for banality to set in amongst spectacles such as the White House, the National Mall, the ever-flowing money, chaos, and corruption. How could the people of D.C. squander such a prime location? Trust me, they do.

D.C. is a fucking graveyard. D.C. is dry like the wombs of its women in politics. It's more boring than boring, because it's tacky as well. Between forcing smiles to the shitty grifter pundits and hearing about milquetoast policy reform, I had started to wonder where I went wrong in life. Don't even get me started about how everyone is a faggot, in some form or another. D.C. is a graveyard, and a small one at that. Too many bodies buried in shallow graves upon too little surface area. Everyone in Washington D.C. is old and gay. All the bars close too early. It fucking sucks. Who cares? I don't. It never stops raining and the rain can never fully wash away the filth because it's just too plentiful. A nuke would be too unsatisfying. I want journalists ████████████ individually, one a day, consecutively. Every day that passes, the living ones get a little more scared. Eventually they stop leaving the house. Eventually they Postmate all their food and drinks. Eventually they move but the hunters keep hunting the same. They are just as dead in the heroin-coated complexes of Ohio as they are in D.C. And one day, there aren't any left. Then we get the rest of D.C. too.

The nation's capital is a graveyard in more ways than its people know — it's nothing compared to New York City though.

Both will burn in due time, I hope.

THE FALSE PROPHETS OF FASHION

People always point to women and gays as the courageous leaders of art world anything. Fashion, design, food, hairstyling, photography, those things. I've never heard anything more wrong in my life – total fucking bullshit. Offensively bullshit. In fact, I would argue that women and gays are the least in touch with good taste. If you were given the task of finding the worst piece of shit painting, or the worst piece of shit haircut possible, your best bet would be to search out the nearest art school dyke. Want the ugliest end product? Find a faggot who claims to have been venerated by his art world colleagues.

Heterosexual white men have created all the greatest works this world has ever seen. If a woman or gay person published something notable, it was first done by a heterosexual white man.

Have you ever seen how the gays dress? It makes you the kind of angry where your stomach hurts. Tasteless doesn't cover it. We've all seen them out in public somewhere. Maybe you've seen them at some club or some bar. The lone homosexual dancing in the corner, sipping his piña colada in a traffic cone orange, long sleeve Ralph Lauren polo. He's wearing boot cut jeans and those Sketchers work-play hybrids. The ones that refuse to die the fuck out. Two other men lean on the balcony below the deejay. Both are wearing only neon green trunks as they hold hands. I think they might be gay. Scanning the room only invites more rage. There have been worse things to happen than the ███████████ nightclub incident. It doesn't help that they dress like shooting range targets.

THAT ONE SHADE OF BLUE

There's a certain shade of blue that no person should ever wear. It's the shade of blue that shirt companies often see as their standard blue. Don't let them trick you, and don't you ever wear it. I prefer to call it "retard blue".

CRUX, MASTER OF THE SWIG

All I really have to my name is brutal honesty and the ability to accept what comes of it. The coolest guy I ever knew growing up was one who said whatever he wanted and accepted the consequences with tremendously open arms. His name is Crosby. Or Crux, when it is called for.

My personal fortune is but a few numbers on a screen, data on a server, exactly nothing whenever someone or something chooses to wipe it all away. And this isn't the case for only I. Everyone could lose everything. You aren't safe liquidating to cash either because cash tears, and burns even easier. You should use cash though. Federal agents be damned, eat shit, and et cetera.

Me and all my friends, especially Crosby, we never cried. Me and all my friends refused to stay on our knees when we're beaten down to them. We were anchors that always floated back to the surface and grass you couldn't pull out of the lawn when bored. We were the strong who don't protect the weak because we were scared their mannerisms might rub off on us. It's unbecoming to feel anything other than pressure. It's criminal to feel anything other than constant war. Nietzsche understood this, as well as some greats before him.

I used to think it was me who had too much free time, but it's everyone else. I used to think I was wasting others' time by showing them parts of my life –

I'm delirious and healing. Car accident didn't leave as much damage as I thought, but it did leave its mark. Admittedly, I was being dramatic as I bled onto the dark and empty road that night. My injuries are bad, but they were sewn up tight and now I'll be okay.

I'm delirious and healing, not on painkillers, because baby that's cheating. The pain causes me double trouble and that is okay. Suffering is learning. I caught a fever from leaving my wounds open too long. The fever dreams are beautiful and I wish I could remember them more clearly. I'm convinced people like Lovecraft were just always sick when they wrote. A fever to H.P. like whiskey to Hemingway.

BAR & GRILLE ON MAIN STREET

I've been here for dinner four times this week and every time I've seen the same woman drinking to belligerence. These are early dinners, almost lunch even. I know it's not my place to intrude on others' lives but then again it is. We wouldn't be where we are without prying into things that don't actually involve us. Conversation is only conversation when it pries. Good advice and good instruction do this too. Outside of that, it's just a series of nods and grins, looking down at your feet or the wall.

She's getting another drink and it makes me wonder just how much of her life she can't correctly remember. You don't have to black out to obscure memories, you just have to be persistent about your intake. Tonight, someone could say something that would break her of this slump and turn her into a patron saint. It's likely she forgets that something, but it's also possible she hears it as she should. It's really none of my business. Our brains are infinitely complex and she could be deconstructing morality in her drunken stupor. This I'm admittedly unsure of.

But still she sits and listens.

I don't drink alcohol. I think it's on par with owning a cable subscription, playing video games, and smoking weed in terms of being a hollow dipshit. Drinking rarely makes a person more interesting. Very few cases exist, Hunter S. Thompson being one of them. I don't drink alcohol. Have I drank before? Yeah, here and there, usually to fit in. Never to excess. Always to maintain a social standing. Did I like it? Not at all. It's disgusting, suppressive to the edge that I am constantly trying to sharpen. It also kills the liver. And the spirit of man.

Alcohol is bad for you in almost every aspect imaginable. But if you're like those other faggots who have to watch four hours of cable television every night, it's probably just for you. Go belly up, loser.

Back to the Grille...

Conversation is an important thing. Soon it'll be the most important thing. The days are coming when all we have are words to remember a time when Sweden was Sweden, when France was France, when Europe was actually Europe. We're being robbed of everything to prove those claims. Monuments, culture, archives, human beings, they will all be quickly erased. But what we do have is our word. We have the ability to carry on, at the very least, a memory of the world before it was thrown into the furnaces. All we have left is conversation. Just pray nobody misremembers the words you choose.

I can feel someone breathing down my neck. It's the waiter and his inability to comprehend personal space. This happens every time I come here.

"Would you like your check?"

"Yes, and I'll cover the tab of the woman at the bar in blue. Don't tell her it was me."

A few minutes later, after I sign the receipt, the waiter heads over to the bar to inform the wino in question that her bill has been paid for. She scans the room with zero discretion and comes up with no clues for who did it. Regardless, her smile still sits the same in between those laugh lines. I stand up, hoping that the feeling of charity is delayed, but it never really hits. I understand yet again why I don't do kind things for others. A few more minutes pass and it becomes clear that part of me just wanted to keep her night going. I wanted her to get more and more drunk, more and more annoying, to everyone else around. It's like pouring more gasoline into a small engine of chaos.

BRYAN PAUL AND THE WATERFRONT MIXER AT WHICH HE APPROACHED ME

Paul is soaking in confidence, or drug store cologne, when he leans into me during a mixer we've both been invited to. Where the confidence is derived, nobody is really sure, but it's loud. He puffs on a menthol cigarette like it's not the grossest thing anyone in this room is doing. People passing by are disgusted, visibly so. Personally, I'm grinning. I appreciate the bravado. He is gasoline on the fire.

"Where have you been, man? Haven't seen you at the usual spots," he rattles off, spilling a little bit of his drink on his shoes. This garners more negative attention.

"Working. Yourself?" I reply.

"I'd say the same but it's been going so well the time seems to pass by unnoticeably quick."

Despite his drunken, uncaring demeanor, Bryan Paul is a man of worldly class. His father ran a construction tycoon until his passing and the man who stands before me inherited it all without a single hiccup. Business as usual. Actually, business as never seen before. Record high numbers, big numbers, and he talks about them well.

Paul works in the field with his subcontractors as a sign of camaraderie, a display of humility that became his favorite new hobby. He loves the construction site and it shows. Projects being completed at breakneck speed, moral on the up and up, the occasional catered lunch. His people are under budget and ahead of schedule. This is how he envisioned the workplace. A successful one at least.

"I wish I could say the same. You look pretty roughed up though, what's the deal? This isn't your usual appearance," I say, in the interest of being transparent.

"I'm a man of work, I've got no time for vanity. The second I stop to think too deeply about my appearance is the second I lose focus on my builds. There's nothing I hold in higher regard than putting work before oneself."

I'm thrown back, delighted by how well-spoken he can be at times. Bryan Paul never ceases to excite me.

The conversation follows this general path. He explains his latest jobsite, how the framers screwed up and he had to fix the mess. I comment. He explains a bit of his ethics. I agree. Giving too much of his genius away would be the exploiting of his soul.

The next day he hammers away at plywood and realigns some sheetrock. Bryan Paul is a man of the people, for the people.

DAM

I don't understand why we look at current events like some priority. We haven't even filled in the gaps of history from just five years ago, let alone a hundred or more. We need to stop and fill in the phantom time. Who were the Greeks? Did they exist as we know? Did they exist at all? Was Jesus Christ really King Arthur? Or was he Napoleon? Who is dating all of these artifacts? We put too much trust in supposed scholars. These people should be examined more closely.

We need to pause for a second and look back, again. We need to stop pretending like everything was written down correctly, stop pretending like everything was written down by honest people. We need to stop pushing forward with a fake smile and perseverance. If history is written by the victor, then it was edited and published by whoever funded them.

Everything we learn is not only wrong, but very strategically, very carefully worded to produce an image in our heads that we can never forget. This works, as we never fully forget, though we can build over top of their framework as we fill in the holes and missing parts. We can make the foundation stable with just a little bit of our time and effort. We can use the foundation to fortify ourselves and keep moving towards what would be the actual path of progression.

Burn down the education system, burn down for-profit churches, burn down news stations. Question scholars and record-keepers, the holders of supposed correct information. The Earth may be flat, or it may not be. But we need to dig deeper if we are even going to know. We can choose to pull the plug now and regain whatever is left of our consciousness or wait a few more years and feel the gray matter leaking, wrapping over the cusp of our lip. The holders of the records must be questioned at gunpoint. Where is our phantom time? What has been held from us?

TOWARDS A
PUBLIC SPIRUTUAL FUNERAL

Deleting social media leaves me with a feeling of disconnection to the outside world. It's one of those of 'good feelings', one that grows within you over time. This is one step towards combatting the usual resting heart rate of panic, that dependence on dopamine through internet numbers, that degree of separation from mother nature. And a mother she truly is.

Everything makes me not anxious, not nervous, but tense. I'm always one-pot-of-coffee deep on the scale of apprehension. That feeling where you're always sure you forgot to do something deathly important. It's not always visible, but it's there. There is something in the water. There has to be something in the water. There is something in everything – seed oil in the food, Chinese chemicals in the air, soy in this, bad in that, et cetera.

Everything leaves my hands jittering and I can't sit down and think without something pulling away at my conscience. Compared to someone's baseline, I'm a wreck, and the only thing I find that consoles this is being an even bigger nightmare to the world – harassment, violence, unrest, and hatred. I hate and I hate and I hate and it feels good. It feels good to destroy everything except myself, my people, and nature. Four feet on the gas pedal for everything that isn't my tribe. For us, it's the utmost respect and looking out.

I hate to bring peace, and especially hate the idea of it all. There is never actual peace, not that we've seen. This peace many seek to create never soothes the mounting hatred inside us all. **Peace is a sugar-pill remedy to man's proclivity for disaster.** No prescription could resolve whatever kind of transcendental forest fire our brains have created. Maybe we didn't create it, maybe it was let in, maybe it was started by someone else and crossed over into our side of the woods.

Maybe we are just born like this. Maybe all the right people are born like this. Everyone thinks it would be so cool to be void of emotion.

Everyone watches television and decides they will roleplay their favorite sociopath or their favorite mental patient. Many of the people around today aspire to be deranged or something, it's embarrassing. It's like they want an escape from the mundane so badly that they'd induce, or act out, mental instability to get there.

I STARTED A FIRE INSIDE MY POCKET AND NOW I CAN'T PUT IT OUT

I suppose we all deserve to have some place in nature. A place where the trees are packed so tightly that it rains twice. Once from the sky, once from the leaves and branches. It smells a certain way too. Maybe if we all lived in places like that, things would be better. Maybe not. Most people don't even deserve a life like this.

Especially not those people who kiss the heavy, metallic knuckles of technocracy. No apology will be given to those who cheerfully welcome a brand new nightmare world. Even now, the most outlandish and science-fiction-sounding UFO sightings can be written off as "oh, that's just something the Feds never told us they were working on". Mysterious glowing shapes and whatever else is just alright. It's really all just ok, isn't it? But it's not. It's an unhealthy relationship — one where the government constantly reminds us that it is the 'tool of the people', that it 'works for us', but continues to show how untrue that is.

Our government is a cruel and abusive drunk husband. The majority of modern people are battered spouses in high-tax shelters. Can you even begin to understand how much 'the tool of the public' has done behind our backs? I can't recall many scenarios where the employee demands not just how much he's paid, but that he's paid a lot, and for things the bosses never agreed upon.

I get it, how banal right? Whining about taxes and government secrecy. Maybe the more we all say it, the closer we get to pulling the knives out of one another's backs and plunging it into the guts of the overreaching. Not likely though. It seems that, much like every other one of modern man's problems, the solution lies in a cut of woods we believe to be undetectable. The solution is always found in nature. Whether you decide to dissipate into it or take it on occasion, like medicine, that's your choice.

Nature always wins.
It has never lost, and I pray it never will.

THE ETERNAL MEMORY CIRCUIT_x

I can no longer escape nostalgia. I have attached emotion and memory, good and bad, love and location, to every song and every moment. I have even seen it go full circle; the memory of a moment attached to separate moments. Miniscule fragments that expand into mile-wide memories upon contact with the required chemical.

How long before single notes on a piano stop sounding like human interaction? How long before chords stop looking like the locker combination of my seventh grade. How long until pain as a sound no longer reminds me of pain as a vision?

Everything is parallel, infinitely so. Everything touches something and always completes a circuit. The circuit always coils back around to me. At times, it stings. At times, it soothes.

Most often, it kills me. Shocker, death is tied into the circuit too. And so I awake again to feel it all once more. Maybe this time I'll forget to recollect those many million attachments.

A WARMER ALLENHURST

Out of all the terrible things I have seen, the worst was to see the spirits of old friends crushed under the weight of the lowerworld. For some, the weight was brought on by themselves. Others would awake to find themselves suddenly beneath it. Both are no fun to witness.

Nobody skateboards to the beach anymore. Nobody has basement parties, hoping their parents don't come home early anymore. Nobody wrestles on the lawn and skips stones on the lake anymore. Everybody works until it's time to sleep and the time in between is spent tired.

I understand that life is suffering because it has to be. I understand a lot more now. I also understand that I understand almost nothing. Some suffering is good because it makes freedom feel better, but I think we've hit critical mass. Much of the suffering now is not a good suffering. The suffering is not fashionable suffering. The suffering barometer is busted and leaking mercury into the drinking water. All anyone can think to do is put safety nets between buildings. Or prescribe pills.

I wonder if all the amusement we had was the product of knowing it would soon end. I wonder if we could have challenged the projection, extended the good times forever outwards. Forget growing up to raise families and all that. How about growing up to start and end bands with your roommates, to skate home from work together, to always just barely make ends meet. It's okay, at least we can still talk about high school and its echoed victories. This will have to be enough until we find a way to do it all again.

BAD ATTITUDE AT GYM, WANT TO SAY THE N WORD OUT LOUD

I power stride into my local gym with a pain in my heart on what I believe to be a Sunday morning. The fat asshole that usually occupies the stair machine is currently occupying the stair machine. He's been doing this every Sunday for the past six months and he's lost exactly zero visible pounds. He's probably eating worse than he used to.

In a failing effort to be kinder towards both the world and the people living in it, I don't slide tackle him in the shins when he finally gets down. Mentally though, I've broken both of his ankles with the sheer force of a well-timed ground attack. Here, in this rift of reality, his ankles are fine. As fine as they can be under nearly three-hundred pounds of fat.

I'm at the smoothie bar now, ordering something I'd never usually get. I instruct the woman behind the counter to make sure nothing with soy comes anywhere near my drink. Soy decreases testosterone, kills your libido, and reverses gut health. She nods in a way that seems patronizing. For this, she'll finish her shift, walk to her car in that poorly lit gym parking lot, and find that the interior of her twenty-fourteen Ford Focus has been coated in three-week-old animal blood. There's a Mediterranean deli next door and the dumpster behind it beckoned to me. One man's trash is another woman's nightmare. I'm above physically abusing women when I'm upset about things, as of late. We mature very quickly in our early twenties. That's what I'm told at least.

"That'll be eleven twenty-eight, debit or credit?"

My paying twelve dollars for a fucking smoothie warrants my not answering her pointless question. I lay a twenty on the counter and call her the fateful "n-word", at a very loud volume. Front desk guy hears this, calls over the regional manager.

That was the day I looked into building a killer home gym. And build a killer home gym I soon did. No man should ever have to conform to the standards of some Planet Fitness or otherwise. Our space is ours. Screaming makes you lift more. The science to prove this is there, if you feel like investigating.

IRONY KILLS

I am not a satirist. I was born into a world of absurdity, through an act of depravity, into the shaking hands of uncertainty. I am the control variable in a world of dependent and independent variables. I was born into satire, into one cosmic joke, and by nature that makes me the constant. Born into a world of the not serious.

When my grandmother tells me I was an accident, I reply with what I must, sarcastically.

"We are all accidents. We are all stardust from the vacuum of space." There are people who actually believe this kind of stuff. Space worshippers are some of the biggest losers the world has to offer.

My grandmother is violently mad, a cocktail in her veiny old hands. This is the last time I remind her about my share of the inheritance.

I AM THE SINGER

Locked into daydream again, tied to bed by light. Music is horoscopes – you'll always, at any moment in time, find one that seems to speak at you, with you, for you. No gluten and never consume dairy that isn't raw. The government made it illegal everywhere because they know it has the bacteria to kill depression. Raw sheep's milk cheese, raw cow's milk cheese, kefir, raw eggs, raw meat. Leaving raw meat in a mason jar for weeks before consumption. Isn't it absurd? Oh lord. Just because something is a plant, a fruit, a something, doesn't mean it is healthy. Life is adjusting to new things, being happy you finally figured them out, and then finding out you're only a quarter of the way there. I've been sending ███████ to a bunch of ████ stations. They always evacuate, always come running out in tears, screaming.

Idols of highestworld shout unto me. They tell me to kiss this song. Which song? I'm baked in emotion. I have been alive forever.

Fully awake now, I stop into store. Half of it under construction. Chubby Mexican man stands on twelve-foot ladder, fixing something. He slips and drops drill all the way down, calls other Mexican to help him out. He says "send it up!" to other guy in their native tongue. The Mexican on ground walks over to drill, picks it up, and throws it at least eight aisles over. Loud crashing bang and multiple female shrieks, drill definitely broken. Me? Laughing, good style.

EITHER YOU STOP EATING, OR YOU STAY FAT

I am the aesthete and the ethicist. I am the alpha and the omega. I am war and peace. I am ying and yang. I am calling girls fat on the internet.

CONCRETE COLORED ESCAPE

There is no purpose to me sharing any of this with you. These thoughts and the routes I traveled to reach them are irrelevant. I hold no weight in this world. The greatest revelation I've had so far in this life is that I'm minuscule. But this is all good news to me.

"I am alone in this world, and it's about time I start acting like it," someone told me the other day. Part of me understood the sentiment and sought to wallow with him. The other part, the larger part of me, rejected it. I did not want to accept that I was meant to stay under and never go over.

Why didn't our parents and their parents riot over Waco or Ruby Ridge? Why didn't they kill cops and raise hell about either of those two incidents? Why is it that white people, who have historically been ultra-violent aggressors, now see themselves as too civil to burn a city down? Why is it we now bend the knee so often? They should be ashamed. No riots, not even a big deal made.

DRINKS AT DAVID'S

David is ecstatic, clawing at the side of the door as he ushers us inside. He's raving about his new patio furniture. I've arrived with myself and two friends, one female and one male. I find this is the perfect dynamic to force myself into any conversation I find interesting without the typical awkward entrance. I control my own group just large enough for independent conversation so therefore I can merge groups at will, achieving my goal, and making myself look like the social butterfly I am not. I am far from that, I am far from okay, shaking from stimulants, but expert at hiding this through numerous techniques. My go-to is simply to smoke. Problem solved — everyone looks cool while smoking. Not true, but true now in this moment.

I offer smokes to a group outside, and get an overwhelming amount of no's from most everyone. This always unsettles me. I find the people who do smoke have allowed another face of theirs to be shown. It's a sign of camaraderie, a bond, a suicide pact if you're so willing.

"I quit smoking, stuff is horrible," some dumb bitch cries out. Wow, such a profound statement. Seriously riveting input.

This argument is tired. We know it's bad, it's part of why we do it. We are self-destructive in nature, especially in situations that seem all too productive. There must always be an element of regression wherever there's peace. This is basic human nature. Had I not pulled out my pack of smokes and offered them around, the balance of this powwow would have been totally askew. I am the savior here, as I always intend to be.

The girl beside my detractor speaks up.

"I'll take one," she interjects in mousy tone.

I crack a smile with my own cigarette between my teeth. I'm sure it was charming to all. I pull one from the pack, hand it over, and light her up. She smiles back, expected by me, for me.

This small exchange of motions and words so powerfully stole the group's attention that the conversation only resumed when the friend I brought, a straight male, prompted so. Staying on topic, he defends my "habit," which is far from the correct term. "Extremely part-time hobby" suits it better. He truly misunderstands the extent to which I am social smoker.

"I think it's a necessary part of culture. It's a sort of staple by now, yeah?" He says, ending on an inquisitive tone. Too British, not cool.

"Not everyone who smokes is handsome but everyone who is handsome smokes," I say with confidence enough to brave the incoming breeze.

Once again, everyone reassumes their best impression of someone who is deeply offended. Like someone who just watched their newest rescue puppy guillotined in front of them. God, some people are such fucking losers. I don't even care about this topic that much.

Not long after, I leave, but not without seeing David's new patio furniture, of course. For this, I would travel the world! Not actually. When he's finally through, I make my way out, carefully sewing through a crowd of scowling desk-jockeys and faggots.

SUFFER OR SUFFER OTHERWISE.

Sit down for a second and imagine the direction of the world below our feet. Do you feel it pointing more and more downward as time goes on? Do you feel the downward pointed Earth? Do you feel the fog reaching its highest tide? Do you feel the ground rumble like war has come, but look outside and see only chemically abused and tired death walkers?

I feel it. And I feel it. And I see it. And I see it. Do you believe it? Do you believe it?

It's simple. Past a certain point, art has never gotten better. Literature has never gotten better. Culture has never gotten better. Government has never gotten better. Past a certain point, life stopped getting better. Oh, but you have an electronic phone watch. Oh, but you have a robot that answers questions on command. Oh, but you have applications to help you sleep with more strangers and applications to deliver your food. Oh, but we have things we didn't before so the Earth must be pointed upwards after all.

Over the next half-century you will see, even more clearly than now, how downwards the Earth truly points. You will see how everything in museums is everything you have seen for decades prior. You will see that everything to be used as source material is everything you have used before. You will see that new advice is never made because the old advice knew best. The Earth tilts downwards until we all come sliding, crashing into the bow.

We are left with two options: Embrace tightly what you believe to be beautiful and run. Hide away from the crowd, hide away from the mess, and protect it forever with your life. Mark off your territory, seek pleasure and betterment through the ways of old. Or you can join the nightmare and fuck everything up, because if you don't, someone else will. Suffer or suffer otherwise. There's always someone putting bricks on the gas pedal. Might as well be you.

If you're good, you can better yourself while tearing apart the lowerworld. Just knowing this, just understanding why you must do it, puts you ahead of the rest.

At least our ancestors had the option to be bored. Ennui, the demon of noontide. For us, Hell ends when our brains stop receiving the oxygen to perceive it.

SOME TIME TO OVERHEAR

As of late, I've been writing down things said by both myself and others around me. The criteria is simply this: it must be worth writing down.

"I'm on a juice cleanse, you Jewish faggot."
  - *Random girl, upon being offered an apple fritter.*

"I can't stop jerking off dude. Seriously. It's like every time I think I got it under control, there's something that sets me off. Seriously dude, like it could be anything. Yesterday I was four days clean and I saw some girl's thighs in a YouTube thumbnail. Next thing I know I'm searching for chubby girl porn."
  - *College kid sitting with friend, waiting for his ride.*

"Can you check out this girl's page for me? She wants to meet up later and I think she might have a dick, but I'm not sure. You can't even tell anymore, man."
  - *Two guys sharing a drink in a bar, mid-day.*

"I got raped at a Farmer's Market once and haven't been able to look at produce since."
  - *Girl, in line at a Food Lion.*

"The only thing standing between me and starting a fatty holocaust is the locked doors of every Pepsi Co. bottling warehouse. Seriously, who drinks Pepsi nowadays besides straight up fatasses? Nobody drinks Pepsi dude. Let's just poison it and watch all the right people die off."

- Not myself, not ever.

"The next person who asks me if I heard the new Drake single is getting their knees shot at long-distance with my Red Ryder."

- Middle School-aged teen, Bass Pro Shops.

"I'm the king of that game, bitch ass nigga. Oh let me see the homework, by the way. Need to copy that shit, baby."

"This would be like the first assignment you've done in weeks. Why start now?"

"Have you seen how much gaming streamers make, dude? Fuck you, I don't need the homework actually. Bitch ass nigga."

- Two college students, school library. The one saying "nigga" is a scrawny hispanic kid in fake Supreme.

"My DNA test says my family mostly came from the Irish Coast."

"You mean Ivory Coast?"

"No Irish Coast, it had the Irish flag."

- Different people (girls), same library.

"I feel like getting raped isn't even that bad."

- Also that same library.

"I didn't go to work for a month. I didn't leave my bed for eight days straight. I haven't hung out with anyone — if I did, I'd have nothing to say. I didn't feel angry or depressed. I didn't feel anything at all."

- Modest Mouse, the band.

"Okay, Crunchwrap Supreme meal and what to drink?"
"Uhh, can I get, uhh… Mountain Dew Banjo Blast."
"Baja Blast?"
"Yeah, Banjo Blast please."
  - Guy in front of me, Taco Bell drive-thru.

"The poor get poorer, and uglier too, and gayer, bitch. Keep eating those fuckin' asteroid nuggets because they look easy to cook. You and your kids are gonna be chemically gay in like two to three years max. Fucking n—"
  - Not myself, not at the black woman who cart-checked me in Harris Teeter.

"Why's his dick so tiny? It sucks because his body is so good too."
"Emily shut the fuck up, you virgin ass bitch. You have the vaginal depth of a field mouse. If anything, he'd probably leave you on crutches. Might just be a grower."
"You're such a bitch when you drink."
  - Some college girls, getting stealth-drunk at the museum, staring at David.

"I had no idea the Halo book series was actually good. I don't even care if anyone thinks I'm gay or autistic, shit rocks."
  - Someone who tied his New Balances too tight today, school library.

"My shoulder hurts so bad. I'm calling the cops."
  - Injured snowboarder, Alaskan ski slope.

SOUTH ASIAN WAR PORNOGRAPHY

Thai ladyboys crush my taxi driver's throat like a bag of stale rice cakes. I'm lost and the summer heat has made my collar wet, my attitude sour, and my wallet significantly lighter. Disregard that last one, the heat didn't do that, biologically female prostitutes did. I am more than thirteen-thousand dollars deep into this night of cocaine-fueled urban warfare and have nothing to show for it. I'm not the one doing cocaine though, honestly, just everyone around me. This alone is enough to accelerate the evening into absolute shitcity. I owe at least a grand cash, allegedly, to someone who resembles an extra from The Matrix. I owe the police department a little more than that after promising a bribe that never got paid. I owe to myself a night off. Maybe some rest and relaxation.

The shift from a boring and average life to a night of dumping four nine-mil magazines towards living humans has left me feeling something similar akin to stress. Like I said though, I've never felt nervous in my life. Discomfort, maybe. My hands smell like fire tonight.

Tomorrow, if all goes according to plan, I'll be on a plane back to America with double the amount of cash I lost. The weight of this outcome relies on whether I find more ammunition within the next half hour. Ask yourself this, and that too.

Anyone who sees vehicles as anything more than a means of getting from one place to another is out of touch. They let my tires down.

WHY WE HURT

As of twenty-fifteen, rates of depression have gone up by almost twenty percent globally. That's three-hundred and twenty two million people affected worldwide. A lot of damaged souls. These are of course only the cases we know about, meaning that there are millions or however many more who haven't been diagnosed or, in the spirit of their depression, haven't told anyone their troubles.

What makes us hurt? What dampens the complex human soul? I say we do.

I wholeheartedly believe that the most damaging blow to the human race is disappearing beauty. Our drill sergeants were right – shit rolls downhill, and fast. Bad mood equals bad outcomes, bad outcomes equals more bad moods, and it tailspins like this forever. Are we not here? Are we not experiencing this due to the ugly?

Rising levels of obesity. People mangled by the many toxins in food and water. People devoured by absurdity, by the downward pointed Earth. Hollowed out by prescription medications, birth control, alcohol, synthetic drugs. Clothes getting uglier and more ill-fitting. Art is rarely inspiring, always more abstract, always harder to look at. Forget arguing about whether we've lost sight of what's right and wrong – we've lost sight of what's beautiful and what's not.

If you don't understand why I'm wound up, chances are you're one of the diseased. Chances are your senses were quietly sedated somewhere along the way, probably by an overwhelming amount of ugly. Don't see what I see? I'll explain.

Whether we can consciously distinguish between beauty and anti-beauty, I believe our subconscious contains its own accurate radar.

When we see beauty we feel as humans should – captivated, inspired, grounded, proud. Simply being in the presence of the visually pleasing inspires the creation of more just like it. At the very least, it inspires the hope to one day create something similar. That powerful feeling, combined with the abandonment of typical modern artist characteristics – sloth, nihilism, regression for attention, poor education – is what I imagine the supposed Greeks embodied.

When you think about an artist, someone who truly understands touching aestheticism, your brain should envision a physically fit and well-read male with beliefs that don't deteriorate the culture he creates. The artist wakes up and aches to understand the world surrounding. He aches to absorb its everything. Absorb the sun, the air, the water. He holds inside him everything he's ever seen. He feeds on beauty to make new beauty. His work never disrupts the order of nature – only adds to it, compliments it. The people of his time are blessed to have lived alongside him. They thank him for making the world more beautiful than it was yesterday. An artist, true artist, makes the Heavens smile, for he himself is Heaven sent.

What is an artist? A man who gets it.

When we see anti-beauty, it kills the soul and human spirit. Anti-beauty – a strip mall, grown men in football jerseys, modern buildings, rampant logos, certain races, the obese – is to ambition what alcohol is to the liver and brain. I believe that seeing ugly feels ugly. I believe ugly damages us to the core, sometimes irreparably. I believe we sometimes absorb and manifest the horrible things we take in through our eyes.

But what about when something ugly makes us glad that it isn't ourselves? I like to think this is an evolutionary tactic, a learned reaction. Are we approaching it correctly? It's not like humans aren't used to disguising responses as other responses to save face, or more importantly, save ourselves. I like to think we've learned to lie to ourselves extremely well. The pain of ugly is still there though, just entering a little more quietly.

What else is ugly? What exactly is anti-beauty?

Anti-beauty, the ugly, the unaesthetic is a mental and visual depressant, eye and mind poison. Modern life is surviving government-funded psychological warfare. When you are down, you are submissive. You have to wake up every day, walk six blocks through miserable Manhattan, talk to miserable people in your miserable cubicles, in-between making miserable spreadsheets in miserable clothes, and every night sleep with miserable thoughts. Should you expect anything but a miserable existence? What if everything looked better? Everything looked better to inspire more creations of beauty, which in turn inspired everyone else to treat beautiful things better. What if everything the eyes may cross was captivating. Large and powerful testaments to the man you should be, the culture you should create, the land you must protect. Surrounding you are constant reminders that you carry the blood of emperors, of struggle and conquest, of former beauty and the squashing of former ugly. You are made of what kills the unappealing.

Scientists and research teams slave away to understand why modern man is depressed. Is it aspartame? Is it prescription medication? Is it debt? Is it women? Is it lack of religious faith? Is it too much television? Is it bisphenol A? Is it seed oils? Is it a lack of direction? Is it gluten? Yes, those are gargantuan contributing factors, but they may never understand that man's central enemy is existing within modernity, within anti-beauty. If you have somehow avoided the mental deterioration caused by wheat and the depopulation of gut bacteria caused by everything else, you've now arrived at a whole new enemy: what is it all for if everyone else submits to the death chemicals, if nobody else cares how the world looks? What is the point of shedding your chains and dodging potential nightmare if the world can't follow suit? To have resisted is to become the

125

unappreciated paradigm, right? This way of thinking is only a different kind of submission. You have the option of going forward and breaking others free of doom. You have the option to live as if you were above all mortals. You have the option to transcend this zone of reality, to completely exit the downward pointed Earth, forever.

Still though, most will never reach even half their human potential. They never make it over. Never make it out. This is why we hurt.

Imagine how powerful it must have felt to have lived in the many previous worlds. To wake up under towering pieces of architectural greatness, things that we still have trouble understanding and replicating to this day. Imagine waking up to the sun peering through colossal marble columns, and then to walk through and past them on your modest foot-distance commute. Imagine you inhale a waterfall's casting mist and know that it will never be disrupted by construction machines. Imagine eating food that sates both hunger and soul, drinking water that does in one glass what now takes a gallon. Imagine we acted against the anti-beauty that threatened these ways of life, earlier on. They should have been taken by the throat and vaporized. They should have been drowned like rats. They should have been sent deep into Hell, forever. Instead, we let them burrow for a millennia plus. Nobody ever poured water down the holes, nobody ever packed it in with dirt. Now we pay the toll.

Comically overcrowded cities with no mercy, no wildlife, no freedom. An outright disregard for the aesthetically pleasing and aware. Spiteful statist abuse, for any and all, except the rats. Political vertigo and the idea that each party has distinctive qualities; no attention paid to the hegemonic demon overlords funding them all. You know those boomeresque pictures of someone pulling the strings of various figureheads? Probably not far off, in reality.

I say we depressed ourselves by having to look at ugly clothes and ugly art and ugly cities every day. I say we depressed ourselves by putting ugly typefaces and ugly clipart on every storefront and advertisement. I say we depressed ourselves by letting ugly people have ugly children and never making that punishable by law.

I say we depressed ourselves by reading the wrong words, remembering the wrong history, fighting the wrong wars, and spending time with the wrong people. We said all the wrong things, we placed our trust in all the wrong leaders, we forgot that we could all revolt when things stopped working the way our ancestors intended. There is zero room for compromise – the modern world must be burned deeper than just ground level, but down into the system of underground holes and nests. There is zero chance of dialing back the damage. Everything has to burn now, right now. The longer we take to end it, the more that future generations are subjected to. There is no sucking the venom out, there is no amputation, there is only submersing in fire.

LONG LIVE THE WRONGLY CRUCIFIED

(Note: I preface this segment by saying none of it is imagined. Whatever was previously referred to as "delusions" or "visions" has become very real, very deliberate action.)

On a night made menacing by fog, this growing community of mine sits perfectly still under its blackest sky. The darker the world, the heavier the mood, the more cover I am given. Passing thoughts of smallcrime snowball into constant thoughts of ultraterrorism. For reasons that I cannot articulate, I have decided to bring the guillotine down on this lowerworld. I have decided to cause pain, problem, and panic for the downwards pointed Earth. It refuses to fold over and die, so I have decided to hurt. I have decided to maim. I have decided to kill.

127

By the end, if I notice that none have actually died, I'll know where I am.

So be it, so be I, so so is the way of things. Sort of.

And so I crouch beside the highway. Wearing full black wasn't necessary, but I did. In the interest of working towards bigger things, I'm kicking off this terror spree by throwing baseball-sized rocks through the windows of passing cars. With the right toss, said rock could kill or seriously injure tonight's drivers. Second to that is a simple disorienting blow — enough to send them flying into the median or at best, into other cars. The remoteness of this specific highway combined with the late, late hour gives me plenty of time to act before first responders arrive. After settling into a little perch behind some maintained roadside pines, I collect fifty-something fist-sized rocks and say let's get this moving.

First throw is a smashing success. Although not being able to see where exactly it hit, the victim spins out dead center on the road. Not even a second later, another car barrels into the first and just like that our desired pile-up is alive. Beside the one driver now dead on his horn, you'd never know there was an accident here. It's that dark. A heavy fog shields a majority of the four headlights. Time passes and, as expected, it gets much worse. Car after car rams into the growing pile. After the sixth or so crash I have to stand up and shake my head around, convinced that I'm dreaming as I do so often. It's no dream. The mountain continues upwards until a new participant survives a killer triple roll-over. He exits bloodied. The tone of his screams lead me to believe there are likely others in the car. This is only further verified by the way he inspects the back and passenger seats, now screaming even louder. He calls the police and it takes at least fifteen minutes before someone arrives. Points awarded to me. Don't get too upset though, it's not over.

In those fifteen minutes, at least five more cars come howling into this impressive tower-pile. And this is despite our triple-flip survivor's attempts to warn them away. It's important that I mention something. This is one of those long-haul, high-speed highways; seventy-five miles per hour legally, but at this hour, tired road trippers and commuters are hitting speeds of at least eighty, if not ninety. Occasionally you'll have a real winner. Someone like midnight Mustang man ripping one-hundred plus. Tonight, a solid two of those rounded this fateful corner, straight into a hot and quick death at warp speed.

A convoy of firetrucks and police cruisers come down the road in brave formation. As if the first half of this night wasn't ecstatic enough, the lead firetruck nearly rams into a sideways car ahead of the main pile. Lucky for them, whoever is inside that car is long gone. The couple small fires here and there are all put out. The lone survivor is taken to the side for a review of the magic hour. Police look completely stunned as they take it all in. Firefighters the same. They have seen pile-ups, but never one like this.

KINGS OF THE UNDERWORLD

Not the real underworld, though. And not real kings. The enemies of today aren't impressive, nor are they scary for the right reasons. They terrify not through intimidation, but in the same way you would avoid someone with infected hypodermic needles for fingers. The enemies of today are contagiously weak. Their communion is a dangerous trading of hard-to-cure poisons, messages and beliefs that will sink the ship of your life.

Our rival's roots are deeper than just politics, and much deeper than their environment. I don't think many understand just how bottomless is the pit that lies within them. I don't think many understand how bottomless is the pit they sleep inside. I speak of the common man. That creeping, sulking, sickly, dulling modern man. He who aligns himself against the still-coming renaissance.

He is weak, physically, mentally, spiritually. He has accepted that he cannot control a single aspect of life and so he submits to anything.

He is always tired, unable to sleep because he hasn't fought the demons of the day, hasn't earned the right to put his head down at night. He prides himself on living in confined spaces, on living amongst the congested city life, on overpaying for the less-than-luxurious. He'd rather rent a prison cell above Central Park than own a nation behind real trees. He's scared to be truly alone, because he knows that years of over-socialization would tear him apart when things get quiet. When the calm closes over him like drapes, his self eviscerates him. He fears what's not hectic enough to distract him.

He largely disappoints his father, fully disappoints his grandfather, and feels nothing but pride in his son. He sees the elders as just that – elders. Ancient, wrinkled faces, ones he knows will soon be gone. They mean nothing to him. He holds the victories of days gone past in contempt. He has zero interest in carrying the torch, in carrying the timeworn blood.

He refuses to lift heavy, to endure real suffering, to hurt himself so he'll heal even stronger. He simulates tragedy through games and movies. His dopamine receptors believe it, too. He betrays his wiring. He refuses to break himself, to cut himself open and feel, to burn down and build up.

He can't stop masturbating, especially to things that even further emasculate him. He has exsanguinated to so many different men ravaging so many different women that he is now accustomed to seeing the other man take the prize. He sits in the corner like a bug, watching and waiting to be humiliated even more. Soon enough, this cookie-cutter pornography isn't enough. He's moved onto the unthinkable, the over-fetishized, the things that could get him thrown into prison.

He can't keep his mouth shut, but when he does, his jaw can't be told apart from the top of his neck. He mixes lies into every sentence he speaks. Poison-tongued bug that he is, destroying the sanctity of man with every unchecked news-word regurgitated. Even he doesn't believe all of the things he says.

He glamorizes the ugly, the destruction of any meaningful values, the greatness we could aspire towards. He calls himself and his tribe "outcasts" but they live comfortably, never knowing real conflict. He destroys art, he destroys music, he destroys good taste, all while calling it beauty.

He doesn't know that when the real underworld breaks through the cracks of New York City, he'll be swallowed up, defenseless and weak. He doesn't know that chaos feeds on creeps like him. When the problems start, he quickly realizes you need a weapon to survive. Which bullets go into what gun and where do they go in? How do I survive the cold of the world? How do I bleed?

SLOW KNIFE DREAM

I once awoke from a dream to realize that I hadn't. And so, I became world-conscious of me and my surroundings. I could see letters and numbers and whole paragraphs even. Not only that, but I remembered them afterwards. There was wonderful music playing. It just sort of poured down from the sky, following me wherever I walked. Others said they heard it too. I was given a laboratory and challenged by scholars and their higher-ups to build a knife to penetrate deeper than skin and what's below it. A knife to penetrate the spirit circuit. They whispered smug assumptions. I whispered smug instructions. To myself, feigning confidence. After doing this a few times, their whispers tapered down to none. Zero whispers and I was ready to construct. I forged the knife from steel that stung to smell. I cooled it off in stem cell water, an entire pond of it. It breathed, moving slightly up and slightly down, like a human chest.

When it looked near complete, I watched as shoulder-high spiders wove leather webbing around the hilt. It all interlocked perfectly, every piece flush with its neighboring strand. And so, with that, I handed it to my audience, in a mockingly formal manner – lain across my two hands, on one knee, forehead down, and snickering. The joke went unnoticed. They were too distracted by the craftsmanship.

Everyone aside from the knife-holder applauded. Knife-holder handed it back, applauded too, then whispered warm into my ear, "only remaining part is to try it," then looked and pointed to a man behind me. The man was bound to a pillar by those leather-weaving spiders. He wore a sign on his chest that read "I RAPED AND KILLED CHILDREN," but as I plunged the knife into his heart and out the back of him, the sign then read "THEY RAPED AND KILLED CHILDREN".

I couldn't turn myself around. I was half broken by the moment, half trying to worry my deceivers. With one liquid motion, a single spin and toss, I cut the throats of every lab coat liar. The music pulled up and into the sky. When it fell back down, it was playing at half-speed. Maybe slower.

A voice from above shouted at me. "Only slow, you listen," and it was enough to understand the point. I was excited to wake up and take his advice. I still do from time to time.

APRIL SHOWERS BRING MAY COWARDS.

I stand at the bridge between you and the remainder of an unfulfilling life. From where you stand, it's difficult to see that this bridge isn't worth crossing, and so I burn it. As the flame works its way over to your end, you scream and cry and shake and argue. In your eyes, I've taken away the world. In my eyes, the opposite is true. There's no room for sandbagging in the reformation.

I hold a handsome blade to the veins of "virtue". A crowd accrues around me, faces contorted. While the many up front stare, those behind them share plans to disarm me in rushed and nervous whispers. The ones who plot against me look over with a different kind of eyes. I can smell their deceit like a dog, and I can smell the fragrance fear. I know them before they come for me, so when they do, I turn accordingly. They lunge, miss, and tumble back again into the crowd. One after another is dodged and never once does the blade or myself ever leave its place. I do this for them, for the both the ones who stare in horror and the ones who throw themselves at me. Once I dig into their arms and pull back, it'll feel like relief to them. It's something they can drown in together. Maybe I'll pretend to drown too. Still, I float back up and paddle to shore.

I poison the crops and water supply. I wait for the townspeople to crawl to the doors of their representatives. When they swing open, it's me who asks what they need. The townspeople cough and spit at me with the last of their energy. They call me names and lay guilt at my feet in the shape of sickly children. Their arms dangle lifelessly and every eye rolls back. But this is exactly the type of theatrics I wished for. When all the attention is mine, I fix my posture and shout, "But it was already poisoned! For so long now! You only noticed because it happened a little quicker!"

Now only half of them scream at me — enough to call for

curtains. The others sit quietly and think. They'll die knowing this much was inevitable. They'll die knowing of their real betrayers, knowing they never fought back. Soon their eyes match the eyes of those children.

The victory lap is exactly that. I circumnavigate the world with a guillotine on wheels. This monster device, created to specification, is pulled by horse until we meet sea, where then a boat carries us across. My tour de la mort ensures there's not a single loose end. The response of its victims is the same no matter the geographic location — unknowing fear. In every language, the cries for help sound the same. In every language, it's clear to me they don't understand their sacrifice. Tall and heavy falling blade, bring us closer to reformation. Every head removed is Heaven closer. By the end of my travels, the last of the list have come to know the guillotine through only word of mouth. Some hide, some run, some preempt it by taking their own lives. It's all the same to me. The eyes of a great rectifier miss not a soul.

What a generous way to have met God's end, and my end. The blueprint of nature and every symbol locked within has shown itself to be true – this much I have never denied. Those who did, early or later on, die in the most violent of possible ways. I hear bass drums pounding like a graduation crowd cheer. I hear it every time I do what I was meant to. The oxygen I use is cleaner than it was before; a gift of verdant elders. The world is lush and removed of sin. I have opened the gates of Hell upon the downwards facing Earth. The iron scrapes its northern-most dirt. Down into it pours terror virility and an ultimate, unbound fear. A world shattered by the ones who once shattered it before. If you had trusted the blueprint, you now escape the end. You escape even just seeing it. The evil are an invisible and necessary power. They scatter across the lowerworld like forever-caged animals let loose, because this is truly what they are. Pain is a small death. You will die forever until you die for good. They, especially. Welcome to it all. Welcome to anew. Welcome to the greater sacrifice.

For a moment, the grand finale almost has me in tears. They never come though. We're not even close to done — a whole list of things to do.

1. Fire to cities and suburbs.
2. Forests take hold again.
3. Lead the animals to the piles of dead, let them gorge themselves.
4. Hibernate in the tombs, wait for time's healing.
5. Reformation.

Only after all this is done can I truly rest. I'll rest in the marble quarters that me and my people built. I'll dine in the great hall I envisioned for so long. And one day, when the enemies sprout from the soil in which they sank, I'll break them all again. The animals will gorge again. I'm giving fat people something to do.

Don't you understand that it really is happening. Do you laugh at the things I speak of? Do you think I take myself too seriously? Will I be crucified upside down for the words I write in the places I have? Forever or just a little? Move, move.

THAT SAME DAY.

"HEAVEN IS REAL," I howl from the steps of the mausoleum.

It's then that I'm grabbed by the shoulder, from behind, and shaken violently. I'm not standing on marble steps anymore. There's no mausoleum of my construction. And to my greatest horror, I am surrounded by many of whom I just sent to the guillotine. Is this Hell? Is the toll of my bloodshed? Exile from the world I reclaimed? Or was it never mine? Do those you kill in Hell not stay dead? Does the same apply to life above?

All for naught is my revolution against the modern world.

An expedition so brimming with grandeur that it convinced me of the divine.

Convinced not only of the divine, but that I had constructed it around myself.

I created Heaven, for me and my people. I even made believers of them.

A choir's song fills the streets and its cavities. The pulls on my shoulder turn into arms wrapped around my torso and soon, I'm being pinned down. I feel cold metal handcuffs locking around my wrists. The aesthete in me is pleased they didn't use those plastic ty-wraps. They look horrible.

After being thrown into a car, time slips me by. I am captivated by thoughts of a cold marble quarters. Not even a forceful removal from this car can ruin this daydream. Does it count as a daydream if I've potentially lived it, though? Have I lived it?

A daydream it must be, I've decided, as I immerse myself further into the fictional. I stand above a lake of fire, close enough to sweat, far enough to not burn. Down below, Lucifer has thrown himself onto a crimson chaise lounge. He lays upside down, feet crossed atop the headrest, cleaning his teeth with the arm bones of Judas.

Thousands of cops stand at the edge of a manmade cliff opposite to me. Lucifer shouts up at them. His voice scares the living shit out of me and everyone else around.

"You WILL jump! I WILL make you!"

The cops stare at each other in absolute disbelief and then, resistant as they are, start looking every which way for some kind of escape. Something inside me knows they won't find it. The abyss is sealed tight, bound by a cement of sinners' blood and the million cursed souls. The walls here are crude and endless.

The first of the officers leaps forward. Lucifer shakes the underworld with laughter. I remain unseen, or so I believe. How many can say they've spied on the Center of Hell? I grab at loose rocks and throw them at the backs of the cops. They can't see me. I'm hitting the backs of their heads and making the whole ritual far worse. Thousands of cops jumping into the magma of Hell. I watch until there isn't a single one left. I wanted to see them all burn.

PLASTIC EXPLOSIVES MADE BY HAND IN THE CELLAR OF NATURE'S WOMB

The police station I've been escorted to, although reminiscent of Hell, is not inescapable. Minutes after I'm locked away in a plain gray room, something pops just outside the door. It's muffled, but plenty loud enough for someone like myself to know chaos is here. A special smell would soon follow to only further confirm my suspicion.

Lacrimosa plays inside me, and it's louder than ever before. Armed teams in olive green sweep through every room until I'm found. I'm scooped up by the arms, quickly taken out, and loaded into a bulletproof escape van. Whoever is sitting nearest me knocks the dust from my shoulders and back. It's all going to be okay.

A quick glance at the larger picture, nestled among the carnation blanket fields of my mind, adjacent to self-reflection and those many aspirations, is a note tacked to a single pine. It reads short and sweet. It also speaks, has a voice. Says this small scenario, although strange, is void of substance. With end goals like the liberation of man and restoration of autonomy, this is but an introductory clause. It's onwards toward anew.

TOWARDS THE MARBLE MAUSOLEUM

Have you ever gotten the feeling that you were amongst something greater than the common man's day, greater than the world itself? Have you ever been a part of, or even known something, that distanced you from the ordinary, even for just a single moment?

I remember feeling it when I was little. Sometimes it would happen when the sky turned dark and gray. It felt like the world might end, and from that would come my time to shine as an apocalyptic hero. Peril summons that feeling because peril triggers the action movie response in you. When the great Hurricane Sandy hit, it made action movie stars out of many. For the first time, thousands of normal people were at war with the world. They wanted it, admittedly or not. The dark sky with his withered hands had reached down into their mundane lives and offered purpose. He threw belongings around, and ripped trees ripped from the ground, and tore the roofs off their houses. Hell, he even lifted an entire rollercoaster and tossed into the ocean like some pool toy. Such a violent and powerful enemy to face for what is only your first war. The best part? Your mind decides just what kind of war it was. Some stood face-to-face with an agitated Greek god, others battled aliens tooth and nail. Knowing the common man, it's likely most only fought a hurricane. Regardless of the shape the storm winds took, it gave purpose to the ordinary kind. How pathetic is it that we've become this hungry for struggle? How sad to have been relegated to begging for natural disasters?

Sometimes you feel it when you witness a bloody car accident, or stumble across the scene of a shooting. Sometimes you feel it when you're simply having a good day. It comes by endless routes, but fleetingly so. Most can never hold onto it. The feeling of exiting normalcy, the feeling of purpose, will almost always slip away. Not for me though.

Now, imagine how I feel after having declared war on the world itself. Even more so, winning the war. Am I though? Do you share this swelling inside my chest? Maybe you do, but only for a moment. Mine? Not even a stir. From this day on, it never leaves these callused hands. I am tired and broken but never ready to let the chaos centrifuge run home.

HIDDEN IN THE BRANCHES

Only an hour or so later and we've reached our destination, signaled by the sound of tires on rocky dirt road. I don't want to leave you hanging at all here. I want no aspect of this recounting to be vague or misconstrued. I want you to understand why I'm sharing this all with you.

After about ten more minutes along the dirt road, we all start to hop out of the wagon. Me and another guy unload the contents of the vehicle, double check for anything left behind, and signal all clear. Someone coats it in gasoline, sets it aflame.

When everything is good to go, we head into an even deeper cut of woods. Once there, even deeper. Inside here is a marble colony of sorts. It's here that we always planned to group up. Looking around, taking note of the growing numbers, I take to the stage. "Well, it seems like we're all on the same frequency then, right?" The crowd smiles. They nod a little too.

"We're here because we understand that today is unsustainable and cruel, that tomorrow will only be worse, unless somebody takes action. We are the somebodies. You may look around and wonder if maybe we're a bit short-staffed. Maybe you think this isn't enough people to bring the world to its knees. I'd say you're wrong. I'd say you don't believe enough in the butterfly effect, in man's desire to be free, in how much he's excited by chaos. Even the people who sit at desks every day are intoxicated by things like the power going out, by storms tearing up the streets, by those emergency test alarms on television. We all want to watch things shatter, but only a handful are willing to kick it off.

Today, we swear it to ourselves that tomorrow should be wounded. Even just a little bit. If every day you take your heartiest swing at the world, you've done your job. Some of us will go for its ankles, its knees, or its stomach. Some of us will go straight for the eyes, the neck, or the heart. Either way, it's all more than anyone else will ever do. It's today that you have accepted that you, yourself, are an engine of chaos, an accelerationist. You are architect of harassment, a jam in the system of order.

There's nothing you're misunderstanding. Many will say it's a dramatic way of approaching things. Many will say that it's unrealistic, that you can't bring the world crashing down. Don't bother to listen.

Remember how you got here, to this mausoleum. In a week, we'll reenter the world as our usual selves, as if nothing had happened. We'll reenter, resume our regularly scheduled programming, and so on. But this time, we accelerate heavily from within. This time, you know where to run when things get to be a little too much. Embrace the death drive but only die on your terms. Remember how you got here, because one day you might need it. Make sure nobody is following you, and make sure nobody else knows you left."

SUPER-ENERGY WORLD-COLLIDER

I see demons in anything artificial. I see demons in alcohol. I see demons in fluorescent lights. I see demons in doctors, scientists, dealers of data. I see demons in agriculture. I see demons in cars. I see demons in activism. I see demons in most women.

I see God in raw meat. I see God in rare meat. I see God when I bathe in the sun. I see God in pine trees. I see God in most all trees. I see God in a few good men. I see God when I breathe the right way. I see God when I stand up straight. I see God in hard work. I saw God and he told me to burn it all down.

I saw a boy and his father on the sidewalk today.
They walked like they had somewhere to be.
Then the sky crashed down — all of it, everywhere.
It was loud and covered all you could see.
That boy — he squealed, he giggled, he danced.
To the ears did his smile extend.
He wasn't happy 'cause his school would be canceled today,
he was thrilled because the world may just end.

THE END

ABOUT THE AUTHOR

"At a glance, Mike comes off like a 1980s teen movie bully on downers."
-    Playboy Magazine

"…Mike Ma bragged about crashing a White House press conference."
-    The Huffington Post

"He's the first verified user to be permanently suspended on Twitter. How he managed that? I couldn't tell you."
-    Mike Ma

Mike Ma was born sometime in October. Despite being barred from his high school graduation, he received a diploma on the grounds that he stay home for the rest of senior year.

A year later, he was accepted into the US Coast Guard. After going through their boot camp twice, once as squad leader, he was medically discharged for sleepwalking into restricted territory during Hell Week.

Now he's the author of a best-selling story with more on the way. Only time will tell how this continues.

FOOTNOTES

A1
Humanity's drunk drive: I swear to God I wrote this section before I had even so much as heard of Jack Donovan or his 'modernity is a drunk that refuses to pass out' thing. Rather than take it out, I left it, because I like it a lot and it's mine.

A2
Asians: I think Chuck Klosterman articulates this 'bored video game player who now finds excitement in breaking the boundaries' idea a lot better than me. I'm not sure which book of his it's from, but I vaguely remember skimming it over once. I know for a fact he didn't see it most heavily in Asians though.

A3
If it wasn't already clear, lots of this book is me making fun of myself and others. I am also serious as can be in certain sections.
Ninety percent of this book was written when I was twenty years old.

REMEMBER...

AGGRAVATION
IS
ACCELERATION!

THE FALL OF CIVILIZATION IS NEAR, BUT IT REQUIRES YOUR CHILDLIKE NAME CALLING AND DESIRE FOR ULTRA-CHAOS

PAID FOR BY
MIKE MA OF THE
PINE TREE PARTY

"WE CAN HAVE
ROME AGAIN, IF
YOU BREAK ENOUGH
BMW WINDOWS"

REMEMBER...

ACCELERATE THE WORLD, DECELERATE YOUR TRIBE!

JUST BECAUSE THE REST OF WORLD DESERVES GOVT-ISSUED HOMO CHEMICALS & TERRORISM, DOESN'T MEAN YOUR FAMILY DOES TOO

PAID FOR BY
MIKE MA OF THE
PINE TREE PARTY

"BECOME CHAOS, BECOME
THE BUTTERFLY EFFECT,
CARRY A SHARPIE AND CROSS
OUT THE SPANISH TRANSLATIONS
ON THINGS AROUND TOWN."

REMEMBER...
WE ARE CLOSER TO RUIN THAN TO REDEMPTION
so
ACCELERATE

WE SEE THAT CHAOS EXCITES YOU. WE KNOW YOU WANT IT ALL TO END. ARE YOU WILLING TO PUT THREE FEET ON THE GAS PEDAL?

PAID FOR BY
MIKE MA OF THE
PINE TREE PARTY

"YOU CAN LEGALLY
OPEN CARRY AN RPG.
OUTSIDE OF LEGALITY,
JUST COVER YOUR FACE."

ELIMINATE GLUTEN AND TRASCEND

"Gluten also attacks an enzyme involved in the production of GABA—our prime inhibitory neurotransmitter, whose dysregulation is implicated in both anxiety and depression."

"Antibodies against gluten have been found much more often in schizophrenia and autism patients than in the general population or in controls, a result that has been replicated repeatedly."

"…in several countries, hospitalization rates for schizophrenia during World War II dropped in direct proportion to wheat shortages. In the United States, where over that same period the consumption of wheat rose rather than diminished, such rates increased instead. In South Pacific islands with a traditionally low consumption of wheat, schizophrenia rose dramatically (roughly, from 1 out of 30,000 to 1 out of 100) when Western grain products were introduced"

"Perhaps because gastroenterology, immunology, toxicology, and the nutrition and agricultural sciences are outside of their competence and responsibility, psychologists and psychiatrists typically fail to appreciate the impact that food can have on their patients' condition."

"Most studies have been run on schizophrenia patients kept in psychiatric wards, where meals could be tightly supervisioned. Patients on a grain-and-milk-free diet were either discharged or transferred from a locked to an open ward sooner than patients on a grain-rich diet."

From "Bread and Other Edible Agents of Mental Disease"
Paola Bressan and Peter Kramer
Frontiers in Human Neuroscience

Manufactured by Amazon.ca
Bolton, ON